A Good Reason For MURDER

L.D.Ridgley

Oak Ridge Publishing
Lady Lake, FL 32158
www.oakridgepublishing.biz

First printing.

ISBN: 0-9814735-2-9

Published by Oak Ridge Publishing

www.oakridgepublishing.biz

P.O. Box 682

Lady Lake, FL 32158

Printed in the United States of America

Enjoy these exciting books by L.D.Ridgley

Of Louisiana Blood

The Dark Side of the Dragon

Oak Ridge Publishing's other best-selling novels

Not the Norm	**Lorraine M Harris**
After Bowling	**Lorraine M Harris**
Whispering Oaks	**Christie Seiler Boeke**
Haunted Dreams	**Bridget Ferrari**

Chapter 1

The sun had just started warming the roof tops when the blue Ford rental car turned down Maple Drive and slowed to a stop in front of the white-pillared home with the double red doors. *How appropriate for a bank president,* was the thought of the driver.

The bronze plaque over the mailbox was embossed with the name *Pritchard.* Lying on the rust colored, brick pavers that covered the entryway porch was a newspaper; the Chicago Tribune, dated Monday, May 3, 2003.

Inside the house, the coffee pot had been filled and turned on by the half awake man, who then proceeded to the downstairs bathroom. Upstairs, his wife was still sleeping peacefully in the king size bed, wrapped up in the lavender silk sheets.

After making sure the street was devoid of witnesses, the person driving the Ford got out of the car and approached the house, then rang the doorbell. A few minutes later the door opened and the man of the house, dressed in a blue robe appeared. It was obvious by his messed up hair he had just gotten out of bed.

"Well… hello. What are you doing here?" he asked, surprised.

"I have a message for you." The figure brought both hands up, exposing the gun, and two shots were fired into the chest of the man in the robe. He collapsed without a sound in the doorway. The shooter calmly placed a small piece of paper in the man's robe pocket, walked back to the car, and drove away.

"John is something wrong? What was that noise?" a muffled voice asked, coming from the upstairs bedroom. When john didn't respond, Helen Pritchard donned her silk robe and went to the head of the stairs.

"John? Was that gun fire?" she yelled. There was no response. "John… are you okay?" As the sleep cleared from her eyes, she could see the open door from her position and suddenly realized that the blue shape lying motionless in the doorway was her husband. She screamed.

Chapter 2

Three Weeks Earlier

Noah Ross opened the fridge and retrieved two cans of beer, then turned the TV on. The darkness on the screen turned mostly to green as the friendly confines of Wrigley Field appeared.

"We want to welcome you to this early season series between the St. Louis Cardinals and our very own Chicago Cubs…."

He walked to the screen door and went out to the wooden deck, joining a younger man seated in one of the lawn chairs.

"Here's your beer. Looks like another long year coming up. You'd think the Cubs would try to do something about being in last place every year… but they don't."

"Never will, as long as the ballpark is sold out every game. Would you?" Robb Ross was in his early twenties, athletic, tanned and wearing a t-shirt which advertised *Robb's Tree Service*. He had a line of fine freckles on each cheekbone, making his boyish smile even more irresistible. He was very handsome young man.

"No, probably not," Noah admitted. "They've only had four games and already they're saying, 'wait till next year." He slid into a lawn chair and put his feet up on the railing. The Saturday afternoon was calm, the sun warming up winter's last effort, and the smell of spring was promising good things to come. The two men were silent, content to sip their beer and enjoy the moment.

"What's the hardest thing you ever did?" Noah broke the silence.

"What?" his brother asked.

"What is the hardest thing you ever did?" he repeated.

Robbie took a drink and wiped his chin on his sleeve. Seeing a chance to be humorous, he spoke slowly, "Well, I once spent an entire afternoon trying to stretch a gnat's ass over a door knob. Kept tearing them apart!" He laughed. "Hell, Noah, I never done anything hard. You know that."

Noah smiled. "Yeah, right. With you, life is a bucket full of cold beer bottles, huh?"

"What's wrong, brother? You worried about something? Cause I ain't working?"

"I could care less if you work or not, as long as your aren't sponging off of me." That was not really true. He had wished for years his younger brother would be more responsible... grow up a little. "No, I'm disgusted... pissed off! I'm about to give up on this damned book. I just received my fourteenth rejection yesterday. Some author I am! Unless you're famous for something else... like an actor or a professional athlete, some kind of celebrity, the publishers are afraid to take a chance on you. People will buy shit if it's written by a famous person... even if they can't spell cat. I guess I need to kill somebody... that would make me famous... a real celebrity." Noah paused and took a long drink of beer. "That... plus the fact that the Cubs still suck have got me depressed!"

"Why don't you kill the Cubs... fix both problems."

"Funny." Noah shook his head. "If I don't sell this damned book soon… get some money coming in…. I'm afraid Linda is going to leave me."

"You're kidding, right?"

"No… I'm not kidding. She said either I get a job or she leaves. I can't blame her. She's been supporting us for three years now. There are other problems, too. I don't know. We're just not as close as we used to be. I guess I'll have to get a real job."

"You got a real job! You're a writer! Doesn't she see that?"

"What she sees is a writer who doesn't make any money. Anyway, she's got me an interview at the bank where she arranges most of her mortgages."

"You… a banker? That's a stretch," Robbie laughed.

"Yeah… banker Noah. That's me."

"You know, I don't read much, but that stuff you read to me… the stuff you write… it's good! Damned good! Don't give up on that. Linda needs to be more patient… I'll talk to her."

"Oh, don't do that! It'll just make matters worse."

"Okay, then… I'll think of something."

"Yeah, you do that." Noah smiled. The thought of his brother fixing anything was quite humorous.

"I miss dad." Robbie said, out of the blue, changing the mood.

"I know… I do too."

"I don't remember mom… but I sure miss dad."

"It was a hard time… when she died. Not like dad. She took a lot of time… it was so slow."

"Just as well I can't remember."

'Yes. It is a blessing."

The two sat in silence for a few minutes.

"Well, gotta go, bro. We still goin' fishing Sunday?" Robbie stood up and finished his beer.

"Sure, as long as you're buying your own beer."

He let out a loud belch. "Always got money for beer!"

Chapter 3

Garland's Bar, located just a block from Elmhurst City Hall, was a popular hangout for the city's government employees, including several members of the police force. Sam Gretch pushed open the door and entered the usual darkness that surrounds the bar in a typical establishment of this type. He paused just inside, letting his eyes become adjusted, looking at the variety of patrons. Recognizing a group of his peers at the far end of the row of stools brought a smile to his face. Someone shouted, "Hey, he's here!"

"Come on, Sam! Get your ass over here. We've been waiting for an hour for you to show up! What are you having? I'm buying!" The voice belonged to Jimmy Frost, an ex-partner from vice. "Congratulations, by the way."

Sam approached the group. "Thank you, peons. Thank you very much. I'll have a draft, please." The beer was drawn and the bartender handed it over. "Made detective, huh, Sam? Good going!"

"Not just detective, Jake... Detective of Homicide!" Jimmy Frost announced.

"Yeah... now all we need is a murder," Sam joked.

"Be careful what you wish for, Sam. I once wished I was surrounded by a thousand bottles of booze. Now look at me," Jake said, laughing, waving his arms at the back bar.

The beers kept coming and after the fourth, Sam pushed his stool back from the bar. "That's enough for me. One more and I'll have to arrest myself!"

"Let's get a cup of coffee and sit back there. I have something to tell you," Jimmy said, pointing to a table.

When the two were seated and sipping the hot coffee, Sam asked, "What's up?"

"Rumors. The department has gone with no homicide detective for twelve years, and now I hear we are going to have two."

"Two? Really?" A frown appeared on Sam's face.

"That's the rumor. You're getting a partner."

"Oh, bullshit! Where did you hear that?"

"Mulvaney. He is rarely wrong."

"My god, I hope he's wrong this time! I got nothing to do as it is. A partner? That just doesn't make any sense."

"Yeah. Nobody seems to know why."

"Well, I hope the hell you're wrong." Sam downed the rest of the coffee. "I'm going home. Suddenly, I don't feel so good."

"Don't forget about Sunday. George and Rudy are going with us."

"Two cops and two firemen… four of Elmhurst's best. The boat running okay?"

"The boat's fine, Sam. Pick you up around six?"

"As in the morning? I must be crazy."

Jimmy frost laughed. "The Coho bite best in the morning."

Chapter 4

At 6:05 Jimmy pulled up in front of Sam's house in his Bronco, the twenty- seven foot Stingray in tow. She was a beautiful boat. Sam marveled how Jimmy could afford her on a cop's salary. Across the stern in bright letters was the name... *Princess.*

"Wow, what did this baby cost?"

"I don't know. It was a gift."

"A gift?"

"Yes... a gift. You ready to go?"

"Where's our fearless firefighters?" he asked, getting in the truck. Jimmy was not going to tell him who the gift was from.

"They're meeting us at Wilmette Harbor. It's their turn to bring the beer and eats."

It took about forty minutes to reach the harbor where the boat ramp was located. The two firemen were waiting in George's truck. Jimmy parked close by and the two got out and shook hands with the cops.

"Been awhile, Sam... how's it hanging?" Rudy asked.

"Straight down, Rudy. You?"

"Big and fat... like always."

"He ain't talking about your head, dingbat!" George interrupted. "Good to see you, Sam."

"You guys ready to go fishin', or you want to stand around talking all day?" Jimmy broke in. "You got the beer?"

"In the truck." George opened the tailgate and exposed the loot; five cases of Budweiser and two packages of potato chips.

"What the hell we going to do with all that food?" Jimmy joked.

"We got five cases of beer for four people?" Sam smiled. "That ought to do us."

An hour later, they were about a mile off shore and trolling for the salmon. It was a warm day with little wind, and the sky was nearly out of clouds. The bright sun was dancing off the water, making it difficult to see without sunglasses. Everything was really nice… except the fishing. The Chicago skyline shined magnificently in the morning sun.

"Nothing's happening here… let's go further south," Jimmy suggested.

"Your boat, el Capitan," Rudy responded, opening his third beer of the morning.

"Okay, bring 'em in!" The three friends began reeling in the trolling lines as Jimmy fired up the engine. As soon as the lines were in, he headed the boat south and gave it full throttle. The Stingray shot forward like a rock out of a slingshot and quickly they were on plane.

"Ain't this great?" George shouted.

"Yeah… this is hard to beat!" Sam agreed. The spray was stinging his face… cooling and invigorating. "Hand me another beer!"

At the same time, some ninety miles southwest of the city, two brothers were floating in a small rental boat on Clinton Lake, casting for bass. It had been a good morning and they had room for only one more keeper before they reached their limit.

"There he is!" Robbie grunted, pulling back on the rod, setting the hook. "It's a nice one."

"Good. I'm ready to go back. I need to pee," Noah responded.

"You cooking the fish tonight?"

"Yeah. I'll call Linda and have her make some potato salad to go with."

The fish was boated and the two headed back for the marina. They would be home before noon.

It was almost five o'clock and the sun appeared to be hanging just over the hazy outline of the city skyscrapers by an invisible thread. Although the sight was glorious, the fishing hadn't got any better. The four city professionals had landed only one Coho all day, and it wasn't very large. The beer drinking, however, had been great. They were down to their last case.

"You about ready to head back?" Sam asked Jimmy, who was standing on the gunnels of the boat, letting go a powerful stream of yellow liquid.

"Soon as I get this monster drained. Damn, everything I do to this thing feels good!"

"Anybody have any idea where we are?" Rudy asked, slurring his words properly for a person who had drank twenty or so beers.

"Way south. That's all I know. We been trolling south for hours," Sam answered. "The skyline doesn't look familiar."

"Put the lines in. We'll be home in no time," Jimmy stated, full of confidence.

They were running along at half throttle. The sun was now setting and visibility was fading fast. There were still no sign of familiar landmarks on shore.

"You know where we are yet?" Rudy yelled above the roar of the engine. He was getting worried.

"Not really. Give me another beer." Jimmy no more than got the words out when the boat suddenly stopped. Everything went flying, including the passengers. Sam went off the bow and hit the water hard. Rudy went flying into the doors on the galley and disappeared below. Jimmy hit the steering wheel with a whump, sending every bit of breath he had in his lungs elsewhere. He collapsed on the seat. George, who had been facing backwards in one of the casting chairs did a back flip over the top and landed on top of Jimmy.

Sam surfaced, blew the water from his nose, and swam back to the boat. When he reached the side, he realized he could stand up. The water was only knee deep.

"You guys alright?" he yelled. The inquiry was answered by groans and moans.

Rudy emerged from below, blood flowing down his forehead. "I hit the damned knob on the cook stove with my head!"

"What the fuck did we hit?" George whined.

"Sandbar. We hit a fucking sandbar. Somebody help me up. This water is cold," Sam declared.

"Jesus… I'm dying!" Jimmy gasped. "This boat's sure got good brakes!"

"What do we do now?" Rudy was wiping the blood off his face with his shirt sleeve.

"I'll get her off. Just let me rest a minute," Jimmy moaned, rubbing his chest where it hit the steering wheel.

That proved to be untrue. After a half hour of rocking back and forth, gunning the motor in forward, then reverse, the boat remained stuck fast. It was starting to get dark.

"I know the Harbor Master out of Wilmette harbor. Let me call Information and get the number,"

George offered. Ten minutes later, the following conversation took place:

"Harbor Master."

"Greg, that you?"

"Yeah… George?"

"Yep. What ya doing?"

"Just sitting here… watching for drunks coming in off the lake."

"How'd you like to rescue some professional associates?"

"What do you mean?"

"Well, a fellow fireman and a couple of Elmhurst cops… well, we kinda got our asses stuck on a fucking sand bar… in a twenty-seven foot boat. We need some help."

"Where are you?"

"We don't know for sure… somewhere south of the harbor. We're pretty drunk, you know."

"I figured as much. There's three or four sandbars down that way. It may take me some time to find you."

"Well, we ain't going nowhere."

"Okay. I'll be on my way in a few minutes."

"Oh, Greg, wait… could you do us a favor?"

"What, George?"

"Could you stop on your way and buy us some more beer? We're nearly out!"

"Are you shittin' me? I'm on duty. I'm in uniform!"

"Well, you could… you could put your shirt on backwards, maybe… nobody would know."

"George, I am not getting you drunk bastards any drunker than you already are. Don't do anything stupid. I'll be there soon."

That proved to be untrue as well. It was nearly two hours later before the Chicago Marine Police would show up in their police boat.

The two firemen decided to brave the cold water and take advantage of the sandbar. They stripped to their underwear and jumped in the water, frolicking around like a couple of kids.

"Drunk bastards. They don't even know the water's cold," Jimmy remarked.

"Well I do. My dick is shriveled up like a button on a fur coat!"

Jimmy chewed on a fingernail for a few minutes. "I did something bad, once, Sam. Really bad." Sometimes, things just came out of the blue from Jimmy.

"Yeah? Like, haven't we all?"

"No. Not you. You're the straightest shooter I have ever known."

"You want to tell me about it?"

"No, not now. Someday. Someday, I'll tell you about it."

"Okay, Jimmy. Someday."

Chapter 5

The four Coho fisherman were passing around the can of Bud, sharing the last of their one hundred and twenty beers.

"About time! We're freezing our asses off!" George shouted, as the police boat pulled as close to the stranded weekend sailors as possible.

"Which one of you was driving?" The man in the uniform asked.

"Where's Greg?" Jimmy asked. He didn't know this officer.

"The Harbormaster got called away at the last minute and couldn't make it. Sent us to find you. Said you were friends. Now, who was driving?" he asked a second time.

"That was Darrel," Jimmy shouted back. "After we hit the sandbar, he jumped overboard and swam to shore. The driver did. We ain't seen him since! The bastard… leaving us to fend for ourselves."

"Yeah, sure he did. I used to date Marilyn Monroe, too. I'm Sergeant Billings, Chicago Police. Which of you guys are on the job?"

Sam Belched. "On the job? You've been watching too many TV shows, Sergeant. We professional protectors of the people don't talk like that. I, for one, am a proud detective from Elmhurst. This kinda ugly guy over here is my fellow policeman colleague. These other two… the bravest and most honored fire fighters in the State of Illinois. As you can see… we are in a bit of trouble." Sam waved his arm at the boat. "And, even worse… we are out of beer. Did you by chance have time to stop by a get us some more beer?"

"Don't push your luck, Detective. Harbormaster said to give you guys a professional courtesy break. Let's just get you off the sandbar. After you're free, one of my men will drive the boat back. It is obvious none of you are in any shape to drive."

Jimmy grunted. "Yeah, what ever," then under his breath, "That'll be the day."

A line was secured and the twenty-seven footer was pulled free with little effort.

"You got a good boat, there," Jimmy yelled at the policeman. "How fast will she go?"

"Twenty four knots top end," Sergeant Billings said proudly.

"Oh, that's fast!" Jimmy turned to Sam and whispered. "We can go thirty. Hold on… we're going home!" He fired up the engine, made sure she was warm and running okay, then shoved the throttle wide open. The boat roared and shot forward, the shouts of the water police barely audible over the sound of the engine.

Sam turned to look at the police boat trying to keep up, lights flashing, siren wailing, quickly falling behind. It was a wonderful sight.

"Get it fixed!" Jimmy shouted. "Man the machineguns, men. Don't take any prisoners!"

"My God, this is fun!" Rudy yelled. Sam smiled and held on for dear life. It was fun, indeed. The police boat, still in hot pursuit, was fading fast and soon could no longer be seen.

Noah put the last of the dishes in the dishwasher, set the left-over potato salad in the fridge, retrieved three cans of Bud and headed back outside.

Linda was laughing at something Robbie had said as he leaned over and gave her a kiss.

"What's so funny?" he asked, handing out the beers.

"Robbie said you two could have caught more fish if you didn't have to pee so much."

"Hell, we were in the boat four hours! That's not having to go a lot"

"He was afraid to stand up and hang it over the side," Robbie laughed.

"Maybe he was afraid it wouldn't be long enough to hang over the side," Linda teased.

"Okay, you two… enough talk about urination. I thought the fish tasted excellent.'

To that, they all agreed. It had been a very nice evening.

Chapter 6

Monday morning, 9:02AM…

The sign on the door said Preston Broderick, Vice President. Noah knocked on the mahogany frame.

"Mr. Broderick?"

"Yes, come in. Noah Ross, is it?" The man was well built and deeply tanned with a rugged handsome face. Not the look of a typical mild mannered banker. "Please, sit down." He stood and the two shook hands.

"Thank you." Noah sat opposite the desk.

"I have your resume here. Everything seems in good order. An author, you say?"

Noah smiled. "Well, not a paid author… yet. That's why I need the job."

Broderick smiled back. "I see. I once had aspirations of being a doctor. That didn't work out either. Well, Noah, you're hired. We know your wife here very well. She brings us a lot of business. If she says you will be a good employee, that's good enough for us. Can you start right away?"

"Yes." He wondered who *us* was.

"Okay… I'll put you with Mary Ann Childress starting in the morning… for training. Be here at 8:30. The bank opens at nine. Any questions?"

He had already been given a brochure explaining pay, vacations and benefits. "No, sir. Tomorrow will be fine."

On the way out, he noticed the other office, a little bigger… a larger desk and a better view of the outside. The name on this door said John Pritchard, President. *Who knows*, he thought. *Maybe someday it will say Noah Ross, President.*

Chapter 7

Detective Sam Gretch, limping a bit from his Sunday boat ride, actually made it to his desk on time. A dusty folder with the words Cold Case stenciled across the front lay by the phone. *An assignment already*, he thought. It was a murder case. An insurance salesman had been shot in the parking lot of a local motel. His interest perked up some. They didn't get too many murders this far out of the city. He flipped it open and read the first paragraph; no leads, no suspects and no motive.

"Sam… could I talk to you?" Captain Boldery interrupted, walking by and pointing to his office. When he saw the name on the cold case file on Sam's desk, he stopped.

"Sure, boss," Sam answered, shoving the file aside.

"What's with the file?"

"Well, I thought you had given it to me."

"Well, you're wrong. Don't bother with that one. See who the investigating officer was?"

Sam opened the folder again. "You?"

"Yep. Spent eight months, twenty-four seven working on that one. Nothing. You won't find anything there. Better look at another one."

"Yeah, okay. No reason to waste time."

"Come on in the office."

Sam rose and followed his boss.

"Shut the door."

"What's up?"

"You got a new partner."

"A new partner? I didn't have an old partner. Why? I got nothing to do already!"

"Yeah, I know. It's not my idea. I have a boss too, and he says *you* are getting a partner. He'll be here tomorrow."

Sam shook his head in wonder. "This doesn't make any sense. Tell me why."

"Don't know why and was told not to ask. So, I didn't ask."

"Great!" he said, bitterly. "Where's he coming from?"

"Downtown. That's all I know."

"So, Mulvaney was right."

"Mulvaney! He told you about this?"

"In a roundabout way."

"Son of a bitch! I don't know how he does it!"

"I don't want a partner, Frank."

"Duly noted. That's all. You can go now."

Gretch left the office and walked directly down the stairs to the basement. He passed the evidence room, the room for storing the various forms used by the department, and then stopped in front of the door marked MAINTENANCE. He knocked.

"Joe? You in there?"

The door opened and there stood Joe Mulvaney… the building janitor for the last twenty two years. He was a thin man with a wrinkled face, and Sam had never seen him when he wasn't dressed in a white t-shirt and a black vest.

"Hi, Sam. What's up?"

"May I come into your office?"

"Office? This dump? That's a stretch!" He stood back and stepped away from the door. "Come in. It's a little early for afternoon tea."

Sam entered the small dimly lit room. It was the first time in his six years that he had been inside the janitor's office. He found it to be neat and clean, everything in order, shelves of cleaning supplies and spare light bulbs and such. There was a pleasant smell of furniture polish that filled the air. A calendar with a picture of the Chicago Bears was hanging over the small desk.

"What can I do for you, Detective? Congratulations, by the by."

"Thanks, Joe." Gretch shook his head in amazement. "How did you know… about me getting a partner? How did you know before anyone else?"

The older man sat in the only chair in the room, grinning. "You want to know my secrets? Come on, Sam… you know I won't tell you that."

"You're a wonder, Joe. Why don't you ever talk to me… let me know what's coming… let me spread some rumors?"

He laughed. "You're too honest, Sam… too clean. I can't trust you."

"You can't trust me because I'm too honest? What the hell has that got to do with it?"

"You got nothing to hide. Every one else here has got something they don't want others to know about, and they all think I know about their little secrets. Some I do… some I don't. Anyway, I can trust them… to do me favors… keep me informed. It's their payment to keep me quiet. So, I let them do it. Plus, most of you guys are careless about leaving papers on your desk. It makes for good reading at night when most of you are gone. Especially in the mayor's office."

"Okay, Joe. If I ever do something bad, I'll let you know. Then you can put me on the list."

"Oh, you won't have to tell me, Sam. I'll know it immediately."

Chapter 8

When Sam returned to his desk, he found a note taped to his phone.

See me, Chief Staff.

He put the note in his pocket and headed up the stairs.

Warren Staff had been the Chief of Police for nearly fifteen years. Nobody Sam knew could remember how he came to get the job, and this was the puzzlement. The man appeared to be completely out of his element, was rarely seen out of his office, and never took any part in any police related activities, except to take center stage whenever the media was involved. Then, most of the time, he took complete credit for what ever event had happened, if it was good… and quick to place blame if it was bad. Sam, as well as most of the other policemen, had never been in his office, which was located across the hall from the Mayor's on the top floor. So, this was a special summons indeed.

When he reached the landing, he heard footsteps coming down the stairs and a minute later, found himself face to face with the man himself.

"Good morning, chief. I got your note and was on my way to see you."

"Ah, yes… Mister Gretch…. Or I guess I should call you…Detective Gretch." He held out his hand, which Sam found to be like grabbing a bar of wet soap. "Just wanted to congratulate you on your promotion. Boldery has convinced me I made a great choice."

"Thank you, sir. I appreciate that." Sam let go of the limp and damp hand as soon as he could gracefully do so.

"You know of course, I take credit for your promotion."

"Sir?"

"Someone else always takes credit for our accomplishments, didn't you know? I remember a few years ago my wife and I were having an argument. I lost my temper and yelled… woman, where the hell would you be if you had married one of those other worthless sons of bitches you were going with? You know what she said? She said, 'Why Warren, I would have made a successful man out of him as well.' So there you go. Good luck in your new job, detective."

"Thank you, sir," Sam answered as the Chief continued down the stairs.

Well, that was a weird encounter, he thought.

Chapter 9

Sam and Jimmy were standing at the coffee machine when they noticed the sergeant from the Chicago Marine Police entered the building.

"Holy shit! Quick… in the interview room." Jimmy said, pushing Sam toward the room. The two slipped inside and held the door open a crack. "Does he look pissed?" Sam whispered.

"Shhh. He'll hear us!"

The man headed directly for Boldery. A few minutes later, the two emerged and approached the desks in the office.

"Any of you guys own a big boat?" Boldery asked. It was common knowledge that Jimmy Frost had a big boat.

"Not that I know of. Why?" Frank Reynolds responded.

"Who wants to buy a boat?" Duffy asked.

"No one wants to buy a boat. This officer is looking for a couple of cops who were drunk on Lake Michigan yesterday." It was hard for Captain Boldery to keep the smile off his face.

"Who in the hell can afford a boat on our salary? And drunk cops? No way. You got the wrong police station, Sarge."

Defeat spread across the sergeant's face. "All right guys. Well, if you hear of anything… oh hell, never mind. Thank you for your time, Captain." The man turned and walked quickly past the room where the culprits were hiding and left the building.

"You two drunks can come out now!" Boldery yelled.

Noah's training at the bank had only taken one day with the different forms and transactions. Knowing his way around a computer was a big help. Mary Ann was impressed. On the second day, he worked the teller window alone, needing to ask for help only once. His new career was off to a fine start!

Chapter 10

Three Weeks Later

The morning of the murder, Noah and Linda Ross were having breakfast at the kitchen table. Linda, a very attractive lady to say the least, was smartly dressed to show off her trim body. Her real estate business was doing very good, mainly because of her relentless work ethics. She finished her bowl of cereal and rose.

"Well, I've got to go. I have a lot of paperwork to do before my first client's appointment. Mondays are always crazy. See you tonight?" The clock on the wall stated it was only 6:45 AM.

"Bye, babe. Yeah, see you tonight. Sell a house, why don't you?"

"Thanks… maybe I will." She paused. "Thanks, Noah. I know the bank's not what you wanted, but it will really help out a lot."

"Sure. I'll quit after I'm rich and famous."

"Good idea!" She laughed and then she was gone.

Noah donned a pair of shorts and a sweatshirt and took off jogging up the tree-lined street. Other than being a little chilly, it was a nice, invigorating day, and he ran a little further than usual. An hour later, he returned home, showered and dressed for the start of his third week at the bank.

He got in the ten-year-old Chevy and drove the short distance. The Elmhurst State Bank employee parking lot was nearly full and it took a few minutes to find a space. He noticed a crowd of people gathered around the employee entrance. *This is strange*, he thought, seeing Mary Ann Childress standing on the side walk.

"What's going on?" he asked.

"The boss hasn't shown up. Nobody here has a key to unlock the door."

"What about Mr. Broderick?"

"He always has Mondays off. It's his golf day. They're the only two who have keys. It's not like Mr. Pritchard to over sleep."

They were interrupted as the unmistakable police car pulled to a stop by the curb and two men dressed in dark suits emerged.

"People, if I could have your attention?" the older of the two spoke. "I'm Detective Gretch and this is Detective Bruin. We have some rather bad news, I'm afraid." There was whispered questions among the crowd as every body came closer to give the officers their full attention.

"John Pritchard was shot and killed at his home early this morning."

There was the look of disbelief on all the faces and several people could not hide their shock. A murmur went through the crowd.

"Good God!" someone whispered.

"You've got to be kidding!"

"Oh, no!"

Marry Ann began to cry. "Why?" she asked the policeman.

"We don't know yet, ma'am. We have just started our investigation."

A second car pulled up behind the police car and Preston Broderick got out. He was dressed in golf clothes and was visibly upset.

"I don't know what to say, people," he said, approaching the bank door. "They came and got me on the second tee. This is terrible. I guess we should go ahead and open for business. Our customers will expect us to be open." He unlocked the door, but nobody made a move to go in. "It's going to be hard, but let's do the best we can."

"If I may, Mr. Broderick, I need to address the group," Gretch said. "We will be interviewing each of you this morning, one at a time. Just routine. We'll come and get you. Go ahead and start to work."

That seemed to satisfy the crowd and the employees began to enter the bank. There was little conversation as people took their places. Noah put his name plate on the counter and turned on the computer. When he looked up, his first customer was standing there completely unaware that anything had happened. In a fog, he went about doing business.

A few minutes later, "Noah, you have a call on line three," one of his fellow tellers called to him.

"Okay, thanks." He put the closed sign in the window and walked to the back of the room to pick up the phone.

"Noah Ross," he said, with empty feelings.

"Noah! I just heard! My God I can't believe it!"

"I know, Linda... we're all in shock here. We can't believe it either."

"Are they going to keep the bank open?"

"I don't know. I guess until after the police talk to everybody. They're asking everybody questions."

"Have they talked to you?"

"Not yet... but they will. I don't know anything more, Linda. I have to go. There are people waiting."

"Of course, honey. Call me when you can."

Chapter 11

It was his turn in the conference room. Sam Gretch and Avery Bruin were seated on one side of the large table and he sat opposite them. Bruin was taking notes.

Even though he knew nothing about the murder, Noah felt uneasy. He had never before been questioned by police about anything.

"Please state you name and position here at the bank," Gretch ordered.

"My name is Noah Ross. I'm a teller."

"How long have you been employed here?"

"This is starting my third week."

"How well did you know the deceased?"

"Can't we hurry this up, Sam? I've still got to pack!" Bruin interrupted.

Gretch stared at his partner but said nothing. "How well did you know the deceased, Mr. Ross?" he repeated the question.

"Not well. Just an occasional hello or good morning here at the bank."

"So you never socialized?"

"No."

"Would you know if he had any enemies?"

"I wouldn't have any idea."

"Okay, Mr. Ross. Thank you for your time. You can go now."

As soon as Noah was out of the room, Gretch turned and glared at Bruin. "Listen up, asshole. Don't you ever interrupt me again! You ain't downtown anymore. We don't like assholes like you out here in the boonies. Get it?"

"What the hell is that supposed to mean?"

"It means, unless you want my foot up your ass, you do things my way. Or get the hell back to the city. Now go get the next person."

"Yeah, sure. Whatever. How many more we got?"

"It don't matter. When we're done, we're done."

Chapter 12

Later that evening, Noah was busy setting plates on the table out on the deck, lost in thoughts of the day's events. He didn't hear Linda approach.

"Oh, there you are. I called out your name but you didn't answer," she said, walking out onto the deck.

"Hi, hon. I didn't know what time you were coming home, but I'm getting ready to grill some steaks. That sound okay?"

"Sounds wonderful!" She kissed him on the cheek. "Would you like a glass of wine?"

"No, thanks. I've got a vodka going. After today, I felt like I needed something a little stronger than wine." Noah opened the grill, turned on the gas, and lit the burners.

Linda poured a glass of wine, then sat in a deck chair and took off her shoes. "How did the interview go… with the police?"

"Not much there. I hardly knew Pritchard."

"Well, I knew him well. He was a very nice man. This is quite a shock!"

Noah put the steaks on the grill. "Yeah, I'm sure. I made a salad. It's in the fridge… back in a jiffy."

Dinner was pleasant and the steaks disappeared quickly. The smell of the blooming honeysuckle hedge added to the ambiance. After a few more drinks and conversation about the tragedy, the events of the day were starting to fade a bit. They were putting the dishes in the dishwasher when the phone rang.

"Ross residence," Noah answered.

"Mr. Ross, this is Detective Gretch. Would it be possible for us to come over and talk to you? We have a few more questions."

"Here? At the house?" he asked, surprised.

"Yes, if you don't mind. We won't take much of your time."

"Well, sure. Of course. Do you have some developments?"

"Possibly. I'll discuss them with you there."

"Okay… I'll be here." He slowly hung up the phone, a confused look on his face.

"Who was that?"

"The police. They're coming here to ask me some more questions."

"Really? Why you?" Linda had a worried look on her face.

"I don't have the slightest clue."

A few minutes later, they were waiting in the living room when the doorbell rang.

"Please, come in. Gentlemen, this is my wife, Linda. This is Detectives Gretch and Bruin, right?"

"Yes. How do you do ma'am," Bruin answered, an amused smile on his face.

"Uh… yes… nice to meet you. Won't you have a seat?" Her voice sounded strange but her face was hidden from Noah's view.

"What can we do for you?" he asked.

"Do you have a brother named Robbie?" Gretch responded. Bruin opened his notebook and appeared to be reading.

"Yes… why?"

"Do you know where he is?"

"Well, no, not exactly. What's going on?"

"What do you mean, not exactly?" Bruin interrupted, bitterly. Gretch gave him a look that said 'shut up'.

"I mean... he has his own place... a little double- wide that looks like a log cabin out by the forest preserve. I don't know if he's there or not. Now what in the hell is going on?" Noah was visibly upset. He glanced at Linda, looking for support.

"You failed to mention at the bank this morning that your brother was dating the bank president's daughter," Gretch answered.

Noah shrugged. "He dates a lot of women. I didn't know she was one of them."

"He never mentioned her?" Gretch continued.

Noah was becoming angry. "Look, guys... you asked me, I told you. What has my brother got to do with Pritchard being killed?"

"Mrs. Pritchard says your brother and her husband had words a few days ago... concerning their daughter. Seems the father didn't like his little girl dating... how shall I say this delicately... a common tree trimmer?" Gretch said, gently.

"You think Robbie had something to do with this?" Noah was even more upset, his face showing utter disbelief.

"Mr. Ross, when there's a murder and we're looking for suspects, we look for motive first. Who would have a reason to kill Pritchard? When we talked to his wife, your brother is the only person she knows of who has had any issues with the deceased. So, even if their argument was nothing... it is the only lead we have. We have to check it out. I hope you understand," Gretch offered.

"Arguing with somebody is one thing… killing them is quite another," Noah answered, calming somewhat.

"I agree, but just the same, we have to check it out."

"Does your brother own a nine millimeter hand gun?" Bruin asked, bluntly.

"No, I don't think so. Is that what killed him?"

"Probably," Gretch continued, frowning at Bruin. "We recovered a slug at the scene. It appears to be a nine millimeter. By the way, your brother is not at his house. If you hear from him, please tell him we need to talk. Here is my card."

"Sure. Are we done?"

"Yes, for now. Goodnight, and thank you." The two men stood and left without further comment. Noah turned to his wife. She was covering her mouth with her hands, a wild look in her eyes.

"You alright?" he asked.

"I'm scared."

"Yeah… me too."

"Is Robbie in trouble?"

"I don't know. I'm going to go see if I can find him."

Linda nodded. "Okay. I'm going to take a shower and go to bed. Be careful."

"Yeah, I will."

Linda headed toward the bedroom as Noah got his jacket from the front closet and went into the kitchen. He opened a door and proceeded down the basement stairs to his gun safe. For the first time he could ever remember, he felt the need to be armed.

He twirled the combination lock and swung the heavy door open.

"Oh, shit!" he whispered. His hands shook as he moved things around inside the safe. The item he was looking for was not there.

"Robbie, what the fuck have you done?" he muttered.

Chapter 13

Back at the station, Sam Gretch opened the evidence envelope and took out the only item they had found on the body other than the deceased's clothing. A slip of paper, found in the robe pocket, with numbers written in pencil: 643-25-3542 and 5-27-73, followed by two letters, S.S.

Why would a man have this in his robe pocket? No answer to that one. Does it have anything to do with this murder? Not likely, but possible. He had shown the note to Mrs. Pritchard, but she was of no help, having no idea what it meant.

"Okay, paper," he muttered, "what are you telling me? A social security number? Has the right number of digits. And a birth date? Could be. Are you telling me who the killer is? Wouldn't that be nice." He put the paper back in the file and headed for the john… his favorite place to think.

Samuel Taylor Gretch had never wanted to be anything except a pilot. As a young boy, whenever anybody asked what he wanted to be when he grew up he would always answer… a pilot. In his early teens, he read somewhere that there were a lot more airplanes in the sea that there were boats in the sky, so he decided maybe a pilot wasn't such a good idea. After high school, he enlisted in the Marines and applied for computer school, thinking that would keep him out of harms way. Then, somebody murdered his father. No one knew why and no one knew who did it. The police were unable to do anything. Nothing. That event changed his life forever.

After the funeral, he requested and was accepted into Military Police training, and three months later was assigned to the Marine Correctional Center located at Camp Pendleton, California. Six months of guarding Marine prisoners proved to be too boring, so he put in a transfer to the Crime Investigation Unit, and much to his surprise, he was accepted. This he found more to his liking and he developed his investigation skills at an above average pace.

He considered re-enlisting when his three-year stint was up, but saw an ad for the Illinois State Police and decided that would be better. He was accepted into the academy and three months later, he was giving out speeding tickets on Interstate 55. Talk about boring. When he heard of an opening for the Elmhurst Police Department, only five miles from the town where he grew up, he applied for the job and was hired. The rest was history.

He was a good looking guy, tall and muscular, dark blue eyes and a face that usually needed to be shaved twice a day. He had worked hard at his police work, managed to resist the temptations that presented themselves nearly every day in his line of work, and just recently… he had been rewarded by being promoted to Homicide Detective. Not a day went by that he didn't think about his dad and wonder who and why he had been killed. Now… he had *his* first murder to deal with. All his senses were on high alert.

Chapter 14

The lights from his car lit up the front of the cabin as Noah drove up the lane and parked. There were no lights on inside and Robbie's truck was not in the drive. He got out of the car and went to the cedar tree in the front yard and took the key off the nail, then proceeded to the porch, unlocked the door and went inside.

He flipped the switch and the room was flooded with light. Nothing unusual… a couple of empty beer cans… an empty pizza box with a moldy half a slice of pizza… the latest issue of Playboy on the couch, and a dirty shirt thrown carelessly over a chair. He walked into the bedroom and found nothing of interest there, except an unmade bed and more dirty clothes, so he turned and returned to the living room.

"What the hell?" He was startled. Detective Gretch was standing in the doorway. "What are you doing here?"

"Same as you. Looking for your brother. Thanks for unlocking the door. I never would have found that key."

Noah sat down on the couch. "You really think Robbie killed Pritchard?"

Gretch cocked his head. "Nah, probably not. Bruin does, though. Sorry if we gave you a rough time at the house."

"Where is Bruin?"

"On his way to the Bahamas. I guess he's had a vacation planned for some time now."

"Good. I don't like him. I think he is an asshole!"

Gretch moved the shirt and sat in the chair. "Oh, I suppose he's okay. He just moved here from the south side of Chicago. Tough duty there… makes a man bitter. He'll soften up in time."

"Do you have any other suspects?"

"Maybe. It's a little too early to tell for sure. I know your brother some," Gretch confessed. "He used to come over to the shooting range at Millstead. I talked to him a couple of times. I seem to remember him shooting a forty-four magnum."

"Yes… he has a forty four."

"You mind if I look around?"

"Help yourself."

"Where does he keep his guns?"

"Bedroom closet."

Gretch walked into the bedroom and Noah went into the kitchen, got two cans of beer from the fridge and returned to the couch. A few minutes later Gretch returned.

"Wanna a beer?" Noah asked.

"You kidding me? I'm on duty! Of course I'll have a beer." He took the offered can, popped the top and took a long drink. "Thanks… I needed that. I found two rifles, two shotguns and the forty-four. Is that all he has?" He sat back down in the chair.

"As far as I know," Noah replied, taking a drink. "What now?"

"We're trying to locate Pritchard's daughter as well. Her mother doesn't know where she is. Nobody has told her about her father."

"Doesn't she live at home?"

"No. Goes to college in the city. Has an apartment with two other girls and they haven't seen her since last Friday." He took another drink. "You really didn't know your brother was seeing her?"

"Like I said… he dates a lot of girls."

"The girl's roommates said she wasn't serious about him and vice versa. Only went out a couple of times. It doesn't make sense that he would commit a murder over a girl he wasn't serious about."

"No… it doesn't. So, who then?"

"Hard to say… just yet. Strange that he's missing, though. Strange that the girl is missing, too."

"I'm sure that Robbie has an explanation. I don't know about the girl."

"Oh, I'm sure he does." Gretch finished his beer and stood. "Well, Mr. Ross, I'd better get going. Thanks for the…er… ah… soda pop."

"Sure… anytime."

Chapter 15

An hour later, Noah was still driving around town aimlessly, trying to think where his brother might be. He had stopped at two different bars where Robbie liked to hang out, but nobody had seen him for several days. On impulse, he drove to Maple Drive and parked in front of the Pritchard home. There were lights on in the living room and the front porch light was on as well. There was something nagging him… something he had to find out.

Before his courage waned, he walked to the door and rang the bell. There was no trace of blood on the doorstep, but the outline of the body was still there in yellow tape. What a reminder. He wasn't expecting what happened next. The door was opened by Preston Broderick. Both men were surprised.

"Noah? I'm not sure this is a good time," he stammered.

"Yeah… I thought about that. But, I really need to talk to Mrs. Pritchard. Is she available?"

"Well, she's still very upset. Perhaps you could come back tomorrow…"

"Preston, who is it?" a female voice interrupted.

Helen Pritchard appeared at the door. She was a very attractive woman, ash blond hair and not a one out of place, dressed in a black jumpsuit with a slashing neckline. There was a diamond of considerable size resting just above her generous cleavage, obviously placed there to draw attention to that area. Noah remembered seeing her in the bank before, but didn't realize who she was at the time. She was the kind of woman a normal man did not easily forget.

"Oh, hello," she said pleasantly.

"It's one of our employees, Helen. Our Mr. Ross," Preston offered.

"Ma'am." Noah nodded.

"Mr. Ross… how thoughtful of you to call. Please, won't you come in? Preston, move over and let the young man in!" She gently pushed him out of the way.

As Noah stepped over the outline and entered the spacious hallway, he was quick to notice the marble floor and the original oils on the wall under the soft lights. The house smelled of… cleanliness… and money. The living room was bathed in a soft glow of indirect lighting and romantic music seemed to come from every corner. There was a bottle of wine on the table between light blue, twin love seats, two partially filled glasses and a tray of assorted cheeses and crackers. A stack of business papers were next to the wine bottle. The one on top sported the bank logo. The dark blue carpet was so thick he almost tripped.

"Please sit down, Mr. Ross," Mrs. Pritchard offered, sitting on one of the love seats. Noah took a seat opposite her. Preston Broderick remained standing, obviously perplexed by this interruption.

"Thank you. I won't stay long. First, let me say how sorry I am for your loss. I didn't know your husband well, but he was always friendly with me at the bank. I appreciated that."

"Thank you. John *was* a very nice man."

"With all due respect, Noah, can't this wait till later?" Broderick asked, impatiently.

"Yes… of course. But I need to ask… Mrs. Pritchard, what did you tell the police to make them suspect my brother might have been involved in….?"

"Your brother?" She was surprised.

"I don't think we should be discussing this," Broderick insisted.

"Nonsense, Preston. I didn't realize who you were, Mr. Ross, until just now," she said aloofly. "Of course I'll tell you what I told the police. I'm afraid your brother was my daughter's latest display of poor judgment… although I can hardly blame her. He is a handsome young man. Your brother and my husband had words. Her father and I have always tried to discourage her from having relationships with somebody she would not want to spend the rest of her life with. Accidents happen. Perhaps we were being snobbish, but we just want the best for our daughter."

"Of course you do. I have to admit my brother is not the most ambitious person I know, but, he is definitely not a murderer. What was the extent of the argument? Was it as serious as the police seem to think it was?"

"Oh, I didn't indicate that it was serious, but it was the only confrontation that John was involved in, and that city detective kept pressing me."

"Would you tell me about the argument?"

She paused for a minute. "Susan and your brother had a date a week ago Saturday… a picnic, I think. They stopped in here later for her to change clothes for the evening. He waited out on the patio. John decided to give him the usual boyfriend interrogation. I was just inside the door, working on a flower arrangement. John asked your brother what he did for a living. He replied that he was the "best damned unemployed tree trimmer in town." She smiled. "Well, John didn't think that was nearly as funny as I did and he told him that he didn't like his daughter dating a bum. Whereas, your brother told John, and I quote..."Well, that's just too damned bad, daddy cakes. Susan is old enough to make her own decisions about that. Besides, when I get tired of drawing my unemployment, I'm fixin' to get me an easy job... like a bank president maybe!"

"That sounds like my brother."

"Well, John got really upset at that and told your brother to leave, which he did. He waited for Susan in the car. As I said, I thought the whole thing was rather humorous at the time. And that's what I told the policeman."

"That's it? That's all there was to it?"

"Yes."

"Where is your daughter now?"

"We don't know. Probably with friends in the city."

"Could she be with my brother?"

"I don't think so. She said they were finished."

Broderick interrupted, "Noah, I think you should go now. Helen has had a terrible day and needs to rest. Please leave."

"Sure, I understand. It's just that my brother is missing as well. You don't think they're together?"

"I hardly think so," she said again.

"Okay, then." Noah stood. "Again, please accept my condolences. Thanks for talking to me." He walked out of the room and out of the house.

Chapter 16

He opened the car door and paused, looking down the street, somewhat surprised to see the dark police car parked a few houses down. He shut the door and walked slowly down the street until he was standing next to the car. The window started down, revealing the smiling face of Sam Gretch.

"Good evening, Detective."

"Mr. Ross."

"A fine evening, if I may say so.

"A fine evening indeed."

"Why don't you just ask me where I'm going next and we can meet. Or, better yet, why don't we just go together… car pool… save some gas?"

"Good idea. Why don't you call me Sam and I'll call you Noah…since it looks like we're going to be such good friends."

"Okay, Sam." Noah paused, looking back at the Pritchard house. "We need to talk."

"Come around." Gretch replied, leaning over to unlock the passenger door.

Noah walked around the car and got in.

"What's on your mind?"

"Have you talked to the Pritchard woman?"

"No. Bruin talked to her this morning while I was canvassing the neighborhood. Why?"

"Something strange there, Sam. Very strange."

"How so?"

"Well, for starters, she doesn't think my brother had anything to do with her husband's murder. She seemed surprised that he was even a suspect.

Another thing… she doesn't exactly seem to be the grieving widow. She was having what looked like a romantic encounter with Broderick… and he was not happy with my intrusion. She also said she does not think her daughter is with my brother."

"Go on."

"Could Bruin have read something into his interview this morning that wasn't there?"

"Maybe. I'm going to call him tomorrow. I have some other questions as well."

"I wouldn't mind asking him some questions, myself."

"I'm the cop, remember? I'll ask the questions."

"I just want to know why he put such emphasis on what seems to be a minor disagreement." He hesitated for a minute. "There's something else I need to tell you. Bruin asked me earlier if Robbie had a nine millimeter. Have you got the lab report yet? Do you know for sure it was a nine millimeter?"

"No lab report yet, but the slug was a nine millimeter. I've seen several of them."

"Well, guess what. Robbie doesn't have a nine millimeter… but I do. At least I did. When I went to get it tonight, it was missing from my gun safe."

Gretch snapped his head around, staring at Noah. "Really! Who could have taken it?"

"I have no idea. I wanted you to know in case it comes up later."

He continued to study Noah's face. "Talk about convenient. Does your brother have access to the safe?"

"No."

"How about your wife?"

Noah shrugged. "It's our safe. She has things in there as well."

Although he was new at homicide investigations, Sam Gretch was not new at being a cop… a good cop. Something didn't sound right. Something was not making sense.

"Why were you going to get your gun tonight?"

"I don't know. Scared, I guess."

"I'm going to ask you right out… did you have anything to do with this murder?"

"Good Lord, no! Would I be doing what I'm doing if I did?"

"Maybe… maybe you're just blowing smoke… covering your ass… or your wife's. I hadn't considered you as a suspect… until this gun thing came up."

"Suspect all you want. I didn't do it, and you know it. And Linda couldn't do anything like that either."

Gretch settled back in his seat, thinking about these latest developments. "So, let me see if I got this right. You think Bruin is out in left field by pointing the finger at Robbie. You think Helen Pritchard is involved somehow because she is not upset enough at her husband's death. You think Preston Broderick is involved because he's holding Helen's hand and drinking her wine. You have a missing nine millimeter gun that could possibly be the murder weapon, a missing brother who is a suspect, and you're sitting here at ten o'clock at night spilling your guts to a policeman who could end up being your worst enemy." He shook his head in wonder. "Well, Noah Ross, you certainly have given me a lot to think over."

Noah opened the car door. "I don't know what is going on, Detective Sam, but I know I didn't have anything to do with this mess… and I don't think Robbie did either. If you want to follow me any more, I'm going home." He got out of the car, shut the door and walked toward his own. Gretch continued to sit, as if a trance, until long after Noah was gone. A lot to think about, indeed.

Chapter 17

It was Saturday morning. The TV weatherman was talking about how it would be a nice day to go to the beach. Noah poured a cup of coffee and started to walk out on the deck. He partially opened the door but was stopped by the ringing phone.

"Hello?"

"Hey, bro! How's it hangin'?"

"Robbie! Where in the hell are you?"

"Ely, Minnesota… why? I've been fishin'."

"When did you go up there?"

"Last Sunday, why?"

"You alone?"

"No. What the hell is going on?"

"Are you with Susan Pritchard?"

"Hell no! I'm with Celest. Is something wrong?"

"Oh, nothing much. You're just a murder suspect, that's all."

"Me? You're crazy!"

"No, I'm not crazy. Listen, last Monday somebody killed the president of the Elmhurst State Bank… John Pritchard. The cops think it could be you because you had an argument with him over his daughter. They've been trying to find you." Noah gave Robbie an accounting of what had taken place.

Unseen and unheard by Noah, Sam Gretch had walked up on the deck and sat in one of the lawn chairs. He could hear Noah quite clearly through the screen door.

"…and, that's all I know, so far. Do you have any idea where the Pritchard girl is?"

"No. I haven seen her since that Saturday. She wasn't worth the hassle. Celest, now, she's a different story. She baits her own hook, takes her own fish off, and shows me her boobs when the fish ain't bitin'."

"Robbie, stop! This is serious!"

"Noah… I didn't kill anybody. There's no way they can pin anything on me. I wasn't there. Got maybe a hundred witnesses or so. Stop worrying."

"Okay, I hope you're right."

"I'm right. You want me to come home?"

"I don't know. Let me talk to the detective on the case… see what he thinks."

"You trust him?"

"Yeah, I trust him. Robbie… did you take my Smyth and Wesson out of my gun safe?"

"You're kidding me, right? Why would I do that?"

"Well, I don't know why. But, it's missing and Pritchard was killed with a nine millimeter."

There was a minute of silence as Robbie let that bit of news sink in. "Noah, I don't know how to get in your safe. The police don't think you did it, do they?"

"I don't think so. They think you did it… with my gun."

"I'd better come home."

"Let me talk to Gretch first. Give me a number where I can reach you." Noah wrote a number on a pad. "Okay, I'll be in touch." He hung up the phone, picked up his cup of coffee and went on out through the screen door. He nearly dropped his cup when he saw Gretch sitting in one of the lawn chairs.

"Jesus! How long have you been there?"

"Long enough to know you were just talking to your brother... and long enough to know that you want to talk to me about talking to your brother. How long is that?"

"You're like a damned ghost!" Noah set his coffee on the table. "Want a cup?"

"Sure. Black."

He went back inside and returned a second later with a cup which he gave to Gretch and then sat down. "Well, what do you think?"

"I only heard one side of the conversation. Fill me in."

"Robbie has been in Minnesota since last Sunday, with a lot of witnesses. He is not with the Pritchard girl, and he says he did not take my gun. He wants to know if he should come home."

"Well, if he has proof that he's been in Minnesota, I would have no interest in him. He can come or stay."

Noah took a sip of coffee. "I'll tell him that."

"Have you and your wife been having problems?" Gretch asked bluntly.

Noah was surprised by the question. "Not serious problems... why?"

"Well, somebody had to take your gun out of the safe. If it wasn't you, and if it wasn't your brother, she's the most likely candidate."

"I like it better when you thought Robbie did it. There is no way she had anything to do with any of this,"

"Well, if your gun is not involved... you're right. If it is... one of you is in big trouble."

Noah was quiet... thinking. "It can't be my gun. What did you come by for anyway?"

"To tell you I got the lab report. It was definitely a nine millimeter."

"Oh, great! Just what I needed to hear."

"You're sure you and your wife aren't having problems?"

A troubled look came over Noah's face. "We had some problems when I wasn't working. I never thought they were serious problems. I don't see what connection that would have to this murder, anyway."

"I have to look at every aspect, Noah."

"Well, you won't find anything there, Sam."

Gretch finished his coffee and stood. "You're most likely right. She's probably not involved at all. I've got to go."

"There something you're not telling me?"

"Oh, yeah." The policeman smiled. "There are *lots* of things I'm not telling you."

"What about Robbie?"

"I'll check out his alibi. See ya later."

"Okay. Take care."

"By the way… where were *you* Monday morning around six?"

"Me? Running. I run almost every morning."

"Alone?"

"Yes."

"Anyone see you?"

"I don't know," Noah answered, starting to get worried about the way this conversation was going. "I didn't see anyone on the street."

"Were you in the Pritchard neighborhood?"

"Yeah, I guess. Not too far from there."

"I had heard that," Sam Gretch said, then walked down the steps of the deck and disappeared around the corner of the house. Noah sat and stared… trying to understand what had just taken place.

He either thinks its Linda... or he thinks it was me. Either way... that's not a good thing!

Chapter 18

A little after noon, Noah fixed himself a sandwich and sat down at the kitchen table to eat and read the Trib. A few minutes later, the front door opened and Linda entered.

"Noah? You here?"

"In the kitchen."

She walked into the room, laid her briefcase on the counter and opened the fridge. "That looks good. I'm famished."

"Busy day, huh?" Noah responded, not looking up from the paper.

"Yeah. Had two showings this morning. How long is the bank going to be closed?"

"Well, Monday for sure… for the funeral. I don't know if it will be closed longer than that or not." He turned the page and continued to read.

"Something wrong?" she asked, sensing his mood.

He lowered the paper and studied her face. "Yes, there's something wrong. Is there anything you would like to talk to me about?"

"Why would you ask that?" She took a bite of her sandwich.

"My gun is missing."

She stopped chewing. "It's not in the safe?"

"No."

"I put some papers in there the other day. I may have forgotten to lock it."

"It was locked when I went to get the gun. You took it, didn't you?"

She paused, chewing quietly for a few seconds. "It's under the front seat of my car. I thought I was being stalked a couple of weeks ago, but I was wrong. I was going to put it back. I forgot it was there." There was a tremble to her voice… not her usual confidence coming through. It was pretty obvious she was lying.

He slammed the paper down of the table. "Are you kidding me? You don't even know how to use a gun. Why didn't you tell me? I don't believe this shit! You're lying to me."

"I told you, it's under the front seat of the car," she whined. "I know I should have told you… about the stalker. I'm sorry."

Noah stood.

"Where are you going?" she asked, worriedly.

"To get my damned gun!" He stomped out of the room. A few minutes later, he returned, even more furious. "There is no gun in that fucking car!" he yelled.

"It has to be! Under the front seat!"

"It's not there, Linda. It's not under the front seat. It's not in the glove box. It's not in the trunk. You'd better tell me what is really going on." Fear had replaced his anger.

"If it's not there, then somebody must have stolen it. I don't always lock the car." She looked at her watch. "I have to go. Can't we talk about this later? I'll buy you another damned gun! It's no big deal!"

"You think not? Well, guess what, wife of mine. Pritchard was killed with a nine millimeter gun… just like the one… just like mine. Now, you still think it's no big deal?"

"Oh, I… I didn't know. My God!"

"Yeah… my God is right." Noah sat down. "Go back to work. I have to think."

Without another word, Linda hastily retrieved her briefcase and left.

After a minute or so, Noah rose, got a beer from the fridge and went out on the deck to consider his options. Five minutes later, he went back into the house, got Gretch's business card from the counter and dialed his number.

"Sam, Noah Ross. I really need to talk to you."

Chapter 19

A few minutes later they were again seated on the deck having a beer.

"Okay, what is so important?" Gretch asked.

"Linda took my gun. She said she thought she needed protection. I don't believe her. Now the gun is gone. She said someone must have stolen it from her car. I don't believe that, either. I don't know what to think."

"Hum... that don't look good, Noah."

"Tell me about it. Do you really think she could be messed up in this?"

Gretch shrugged. "Maybe. Do you have a photo of her I could borrow?"

"A photo? Why?"

"Noah, I'm not ready to talk about it yet, but we're checking phone records of everyone involved. Let's just say there are some unanswered questions concerning your wife. I really need that photo."

After Gretch left, Noah went into the bedroom, got a duffle bag from the closet and packed enough clothes for a couple of days. Then he wrote Linda a note and put it on her pillow.

Linda,

I don't know what is going on with you, but I know something is. Something bad. I need to be alone to think. If there is something you need to tell me, I'll be at Robbie's.

Chapter 20

At ten the next morning, Noah parked his car in the lot and went up the steps to enter the funeral home. There was a huge crowd in the outer room, most of whom he had never seen before. He recognized the familiar face of a co-worker and approached him.

"Big crowd, huh?"

"Hi, Noah. Yeah… a lot of people. He was a well known man. We'd better go inside and get a seat."

They found seats near the back of the room. The casket was grand; the center piece of at least a hundred flower arrangements. The family was seated to one side and Noah could see Preston Broderick sitting next to Mrs. Pritchard who was holding the hand of a young woman. The missing daughter had been found. The music started, appropriately sad.

"Looks like Broderick is going to make out alright," his friend commented. "The bank presidency and the gorgeous Helen Pritchard, huh?"

"Yeah, not bad," Noah agreed. "Not bad at all."

The service was long with several eulogies. He chose not to go to the cemetery, the ceremony causing him to be depressed enough. Instead, he drove out to Robbie's cabin and took a nap in the hammock on the front porch.

Around six, he found a small pizza in the freezer, cooked it in the oven and went back to the front porch to eat. He had just finished it and was on his second beer when Gretch's car pulled up the drive.

"Got another one of those?" Gretch asked, sitting beside Noah on the steps.

"You here to arrest me?"

"No… I'm here for the free beer."

"Okay. In that case, you can have one." Noah went inside and returned with the can, giving it to the detective. He took the can, holding it between his thumb and little finger, as if he were holding a stein by an imaginary handle.

"What's going on? Did they find my gun?"

"Nope, no gun. Just thought I give you the latest." Gretch took a long drink. "Man, that's good beer!"

"What's so special about the beer?"

"It's free." He paused. "Sometimes this job really sucks, Noah."

"Did you talk to Bruin?"

"You sure got a lot of questions."

"Well?"

"Can't find Bruin. He never checked in to the hotel… in fact, he never got on the plane. He is not in the Bahamas."

"I knew it!"

"You knew what?"

Noah paused. He wasn't really sure what he knew. "Okay, so what do you think?"

"When we came to your house, that first night, did you notice anything… strange… when Bruin and your wife were introduced?"

"No, but I wasn't looking at them."

"Well, I could be wrong… but I thought at the time, that perhaps this was not the first time they had met. Just a look on your wife's face. I'm usually pretty good at picking up on things like that."

"Linda… and Bruin? What does that mean?"

"I don't know. Maybe nothing. Anyway, I've got the Feds looking for Bruin." The policeman took another drink. "I've got more bad news, I'm afraid."

"What now?" Noah was getting even more depressed.

Gretch was staring off in the distance. "We checked John Pritchard's credit cards and phone records for the past few months. Seems he was calling your wife's cell phone several times a day. Also, he was renting a hotel room in the city a couple of times a week. The desk clerk identified your wife's photo as his companion. I'm sorry."

Noah leaned over and put his face in his hands. "My God! I don't believe this." He shook his head as if trying to make it all go away. "Linda and Pritchard? Wow," he whispered. He fought back the tears, taking a deep breath. His mind was a whirlwind of thoughts. "Well, talk about motives. It could be Linda. It could be Helen Pritchard. It could be Broderick. It could be Bruin. It could be me. We're all great suspects… but it looks like I'm the only one that's not been getting laid!"

"Yeah, seems that way. You all had a good reason for murder, if there is such a thing. You all might just have wanted Pritchard dead… except Bruin. Him, I don't figure. Besides, he was with me when the murder was committed. We were having breakfast. On the other hand, if you knew about your wife, I'd say you had the best motive… but I don't think you knew."

"I should have. I must be a complete fool."

"Don't feel bad. My ex-wife was doing my partner for over a year before I found out."

"What did you do?"

"Moved out, just like you did. I wanted to kill the guy, but I didn't."

"I didn't kill anybody either, Sam."

There was a minute of silence.

"Are you writing about this? You doing a book?"

Noah's head snapped up. "How do you know about my writing?"

"Well, when I talked to your wife, she said you were trying to get a book published, and that you used to say you'd have to kill somebody in order to get it done."

"Jesus, it was a joke! It's not a joke anymore. She's trying to put the blame on me?"

"Maybe." Gretch stood and started to walk towards his car. "I'll be in touch. Don't go anywhere… out of town, I mean." He held up the beer can. "I'll finish this in the car."

Noah watched the police car disappear down the lane, leaving him full of sadness and grief. He had loved Linda. He had just lost Linda. *My God, what will I do?* A cricket started chirping under the porch.

"Shut up," he muttered, throwing his beer can at the sound.

Chapter 21

Sam Gretch returned to the police station after talking to Noah, but instead of going to his office he went straight to the basement, beyond the evidence room, and once again, knocked on the door. It opened.

"Again? What now?"

"Joe… I need a favor."

"Come in, Sam."

It was a little past ten p.m. when the pick up drove up the lane and parked beside Noah's car. The young man got out, approached the house, and went inside.

"Noah? You here?"

"Turn on the lights, dummy, before you trip over me," Noah answered, his voice slurred.

Robbie flipped the switch and the room was filled with brightness. Noah was sitting on the couch, obviously very drunk. There were several empty beer cans on the floor and on the coffee table.

"Damn, you scared the hell out of me. Speaking of hell, you look like hell!"

"So what! I got the right to look like hell. My wife's been screwing another man, I'm probably going to prison for a murder I didn't commit… and my brother is off fishin' and lookin' at his girl friend's tits while all this is going on," followed by a belch.

"Any beer left?" Robbie asked calmly.

Noah waved a hand toward the kitchen. “Yeah, I think so.”

“Okay, I’ll be right back and you can tell me all about it.”

Chapter 22

The bank was busy and that was a good thing. When the bank was busy, Noah was busy… and not dwelling on his personal problems. He looked up from a customer to notice a group of people entering the conference room.

"What's going on?" he whispered, turning to a fellow worker.

"That's the board of directors. I assume they're going to make Broderick's new position official."

Noah turned back to his window and was surprised to find Detective Gretch standing there. He was not there to do banking.

"I need you to come with me. I won't make a scene if you don't."

Noah nodded. He took a deep breath, put the closed sign in front of the teller window, and walked around the counter to join Gretch. Silently, the two men walked out of the bank.

Gretch opened the passenger door of the unidentified police car. "Get in. We have to go to the station."

"Why do we have to go to the station?"

"We found the murder weapon. A mailman found it in a drop box two blocks from the Pritchard's. Guess whose prints are on it."

"You tell me."

"Yours."

Noah slumped in the seat. "I didn't kill Pritchard, Sam. I didn't kill anyone. How the hell do you know they're my prints anyway?"

"Beer can. You gave it to me."

"Remind me to give you another one some day! I tell you, I didn't kill John Pritchard!"

"Maybe not... maybe yes. Right now, the evidence says you did."

"Am I under arrest?"

"Not yet. It ain't quite that simple. In fact, it's getting damned complicated. First, Pritchard tried to break it off with your wife a month ago. The hotel clerk said they had a big fight in the lobby and she threatened him. Then our investigation on Bruin turned up something strange. He made three large bank deposits in the last three weeks, totaling ninety thousand dollars. Withdrew it all the day he was supposed to go on vacation. Now he has disappeared."

"So you do think he's involved?"

"Well, it did get me thinking... so I checked financial transactions of everybody I could think of."

"And?"

"Preston Broderick had a $50,000 cashier's check issued from a bank in Plainfield a week ago Friday. Helen Pritchard withdrew $30,000 from her savings account on Tuesday last, and a Mrs. Linda Ross took a $10,000 advance form Parkinson Real-estate Company. Total... $90,000. I don't believe in coincidences. I think three people paid Bruin to do something. You didn't pay. That's the only reason why you're not under arrest...yet."

"If they paid Bruin... to kill Pritchard, how in the hell did they get together?"

"I have a theory. Want to hear it?"

"By all means!"

"Okay. Helen Pritchard, Preston Broderick and your wife... they all had a reason for wanting John Pritchard dead. Some how... and that's the great mystery… Bruin gets into the picture. It looks like they all paid him a fee… to kill Pritchard. But maybe they didn't know about each other. I figure Bruin was playing each one for as much as they could afford. That's why the amounts differ. Then last Monday… somebody kills Pritchard. But it wasn't Bruin. He figures that everybody will think it was him, so he runs… as originally planned…. with the money."

"That's a stretch!"

"Yeah, maybe. I told you it was a theory."

"So, if it wasn't Bruin… then who?"

"That brings me back to you… or your brother. I'm waiting on a call from Minnesota. If your brother's alibi checks out, then I have no choice except to arrest you. We're going to wait at the station."

Chapter 23

The Police Station was located in the rear of City Hall. Noah was ushered into an interview room with an uncomfortable chair and a plain steel table. Not being familiar with such facilities, he was surprised to find them bolted to the floor.

Gretch promised he would be back soon and disappeared, heading straight for the captain's office. He burst through the door.

"Tell me again… why did you agree to take Bruin?"

"Sam… I told you, it was not my decision. I was given him on a platter, so to speak."

"Who? Who wanted him here?"

"I don't know. Somebody who has pull with the top brass. I was ordered not to ask questions."

"What's the story in Chicago? Why did he leave there?"

"Rumors. Just rumors. There was never any proof of anything."

"So we got a bad cop. You gave me a bad cop partner."

"Well, he's gone now. Let's just let it be."

"He figures in the Pritchard murder, you know."

"Just follow the evidence, Sam. Wherever it takes you. That's what we do."

"The evidence says Noah Ross did it. My gut tells me that he didn't. I think somebody is setting him up."

"Maybe so. It will all come out. It always does."

"No, not always. The jails are full of innocent people."

"Sam... you're beating a dead horse. Do your job."

"Can't you think of anything more original to say?"

"Yeah...get the fuck out of my office."

Noah stood up and walked around the small interview room, taking note of the large mirror. *Just like in the movies*, he thought. *I wonder who is on the other side looking at me.* The door opened and Gretch entered.

"Your brother's alibi checked out. Deputy Sheriff up there said he quit counting at eight people who were with your brother in Ely. I've got no choice, Noah. I'm officially placing you under arrest for the murder of John Pritchard. You have the right to remain silent. You..."

"Stop it. Consider it said." Noah collapsed on the chair. "I can't believe this is happening! What about Bruin?"

"That's a different matter. I'll deal with him later. Why don't you just tell me all about it. Tell me how it happened. You found out Pritchard was doing your wife, didn't you? Went off the deep end?"

Noah sensed the different demeanor in the policeman and for a moment was puzzled. Then it became clear why. Of course, they were being watched... by his superiors. Gretch had to do his job.

"I want to call my lawyer."

"Fine! Call your lawyer. I won't be able to help you once he's here."

"It's a she... not a he."

"Oh, that makes a big difference. Okay, then you'll be going down to Booking. Good luck!"

He was back in the same room. It had been over two hours since Gretch had left. He had been fingerprinted, photographed, searched and clothed in an orange jumpsuit with a large "P" on the back. He went through the entire process in a daze. Beatrice had said she would be right there. Right there. That was over an hour ago. Finally, the door opened and a uniformed policeman let her in.

"Noah… sorry for taking so long. I was meeting with Sam Gretch." Beatrice Martin was an attractive woman; a full figure, carefully styled black hair and a pretty smile. Noah had dated her in High School, before she left for college to get her degree and become part of her father's law firm. "I must say, it appears they have a pretty strong case against you. First, tell me you're innocent!" She sat down at the table and opened her briefcase.

"Of course, I'm innocent!"

"Okay… then, let's start at the top. Don't leave anything out. We have got our work cut out for us on this one." She took out a yellow legal pad.

"You're not making me feel good."

"There's a lot of evidence… and none of it is good."

Noah nodded. "I know. In the meantime, can you get me out of here?"

"I'm going to try, but don't get your hopes up."

Chapter 24

The arraignment hearing was set for two the next afternoon. At ten that morning, the state prosecutor and his assistant came to interview Noah Ross.

"If I blink, don't answer the question," Beatrice had instructed.

The prosecutor looked as if he had been cast in the roll by a movie executive.

"Mr. Ross, I'm Gordon Sterns. I will be the prosecuting chair and this is Phillip Hamm. He will be assisting. Are you being treated alright here?"

"Yeah, just like on vacation," Noah answered bitterly.

"Are you prepared to make a statement?"

"Yes. I had absolutely nothing to do with the death of John Pritchard."

"How do you explain the murder weapon being your gun?"

Beatrice blinked.

"I have no explanation for that."

"Were you aware that your wife and John Pritchard were having an affair?"

"Not until after his death. The police told me. Sam Gretch, to be exact."

"How do you account for being at the Pritchard residence the morning of the shooting?"

"I wasn't at the Pritchard's residence," Noah responded, surprised.

"We have a witness that says you were."

"Then they are mistaken."

"Why did you shoot twice? Were you not sure of the first shot?"

Beatrice blinked.

"That was a cheap shot. You really think I'm that stupid?"

"Mr. Ross, we have motive, we have the weapon, and we have a witness that has placed you at the scene. Perhaps you should discuss the possibility of a plea with your attorney."

"Are you offering us one?" Beatrice asked immediately.

"We would consider it," Sterns said. "A husband that just found out his wife was cheating… going off the deep end and doing something he would regret for the rest of his life. A jury might take a sympathetic view."

"Damn it, I didn't do it! I am not going to take any plea just to make your job easier! I am not guilty!"

"Talk to him, Ms. Martin. Explain the situation. We're talking about Man-One versus life. We'll see you at the bail hearing." The two men left the room.

"Manslaughter, first degree… that's fifteen to twenty. Probably out in less than ten. First degree murder… probably life."

"Beatrice…I didn't kill the man. Somehow, we have to find a way to prove it!"

"What about this witness? You didn't tell me about any witness."

"I don't remember seeing anyone on my run that morning. I never got any closer than three blocks to the Pritchard house."

"Okay. Give me the key to your place. I'll have to get you some suitable clothes for the hearing tomorrow. Linda may not let me in."

"Yeah… like I have the key. Everything I had is in a big brown envelope, remember? Call Robbie if she won't let you in. He has a key."

Sam Gretch had filled out the arrest papers and was filing a Felony Complaint at his desk when the phone rang.

"Gretch."

"Mulvaney. I called a fellow I know in Bruin's old precinct. This is all off the record, now. Bruin was suspected to be on the take over there. Internal Affairs had been investigating him for months, then suddenly, they dropped the case, and Bruin left. That's when he showed up here."

"So, he has friends in high places. Probably just as dirty," Sam mumbled.

"That's not all. There was a strong rumor a while back that Bruin's gun was for hire. Whether or not he actually whacked anyone, my source wasn't sure. That's all I got."

"Thanks Joe. I appreciate the info."

"You're on my list, now, Sam."

"Yeah, I suppose I am."

"Oh, I almost forgot. Hold on to you hat. Bruin is our mayor's second cousin."

"No way!"

"Yes, way."

"Holy shit!"

Chapter 25

The Criminal Court room on the top floor of City Hall was a madhouse of drunks, prostitutes and a variety of other drug-related criminals, all trying to get out of jail. When it came Noah's turn, the bailiff read the charges of first degree murder and the interest of the judge picked up. He didn't get many murder cases. In fact, this was his first one.

"How does the defendant plead?" he asked.

"Not guilty, Your Honor," Beatrice answered.

"We would like the defendant remanded without bail, Your Honor," the prosecutor stated.

"Your Honor, my client has never been arrested before… not even for a traffic ticket. He is not a flight risk. He doesn't even have a passport. He is not a criminal. We feel his life would be in danger in jail."

"Mr. Sterns, do you have reason to consider the defendant a flight risk?"

"Well, he is being charged with murder, Your Honor."

"That doesn't mean he'll run. Bail is set at $100,000. Grand Jury convenes in five days. Next case!"

The bailiff whisked Noah toward the door leading back to the holding cells. "What does that mean, Beatrice?" he asked over his shoulder.

"I'll have you out in a couple of hours. We caught a break!"

Three hours later, they were in Beatrice's car going back to the bank to pick up his car.

"I don't have a $100,000. Where did you get my bail money?"

"A bondsman. The firm put up your ten percent deposit."

"I don't even have ten thousand dollars. Now what?"

"Noah, we can work out the details later. Yes, you are going to owe us lots of money. There is no way around that, I'm afraid. You did get yourself arrested, you know. Right now, let's concentrate on getting you acquitted!"

"God, what a mess! I've never even been in handcuffs before." He stared out the window, saying no more, lost in a thousand unpleasant thoughts.

Chapter 26

Sam Gretch entered the bank and paused for moment, looking around. Business as usual. No evidence that the head man had just recently been murdered. He remembered something his father used to say. 'A person is remembered by most about as long as it takes to fill the hole… when you pull your finger out of a bucket of water.' "I guess so," he muttered softly.

He knocked on the open door of the bank president's office, now occupied by Preston Broderick, who looked up from the report he was reading.

"Oh, hi, Detective. Come in. What can I do for you?"

"Just a few questions, sir… if I might?"

"Of course. What a shock about Mr. Ross. I would never have thought…"

"Yes. It is a shock, for sure. But then, evidence rarely lies… and the evidence says he did it." Sam replied, unconvincingly, taking a chair.

"You don't believe the evidence?"

"Well, let's just say I still have a lot of unanswered questions. For example, Noah Ross is not the only one to have a reason for wanting John Pritchard out of the picture. Even you seemed to have benefited."

Broderick stiffened. "Me! I didn't have anything to do with any of this!"

"Did you know Detective Bruin… prior to our investigation?" Sam decided to go fishing.

Broderick glared at the policeman. “Do I need an attorney?” he gritted.

Sam shrugged. “I don’t know, do you?”

Broderick’s eyes were reduced to mere slits. “You are out of line, Detective. Get off my back!”

“You didn’t answer my question. Did you know Detective Bruin?”

“Get out of my office. You have any more to say to me, call my lawyer. I don’t have to answer your stupid questions.” Broderick rose and went to the door. “Get out… now.”

“Okay, sure. Just one more question… how well do you know the mayor?”

“Go to hell!” Broderick walked out of the office and disappeared into a conference room, shutting the door.

Chapter 27

"I never knew just how bad it is… being in jail."

"I spent one night there, when I got my DUI," Robbie responded. The two brothers were sitting on the front steps of Robbie's cabin. "No, it sure ain't fun."

"Fun? There were four other guys in the holding cell. One of them kept wanting to show me the tattoo on his pecker. Another was trying to sell me drugs! Now, you tell me, how could they still have drugs on them in jail?"

Robbie shrugged. "Probably had it up his ass when he was arrested."

"I suppose. Man, what a nightmare. The thought of being in prison is terrifying."

"Do you have any idea how the killer got hold of your gun?"

"Linda said she had it under the front seat of the car. I don't know whether to believe her or not. She said somebody had to steal it. I don't think so."

"I suppose they could have. Stolen it, I mean."

"Well, it's possible, just not probable. Then to find out she's been screwing Pritchard. Man that blew me away."

Robbie nodded. "Yeah, I know."

"No, you don't know. You just think you do."

"Whatever. What happens next?"

"Beatrice is working on my case for the Grand Jury. She's pretty sure I'll be indicted. Then we go to trial… then they send my ass to prison. God,

Robbie, I don't know what to do! Somebody is framing me…and I don't know why!"

"I don't know what to say, brother."

The cricket under the steps started to chirp again.

"See? Even the damn cricket thinks I'm guilty."

Chapter 28

Linda Ross finished putting the contract papers for her last sale in order, closed the file folder and put it in the drawer. When she turned around, she was startled to find Sam Gretch standing in the doorway of her office.

"Mr. Gretch. I didn't hear you come in. You scared me!"

"Sorry, Mrs. Ross. I didn't mean to do that. I knocked… perhaps you didn't hear me."

"No… I didn't." She sat at her desk. "More questions?"

"A couple. Do you believe your husband killed John Pritchard?"

"No. I don't. He couldn't do that."

Sam was silent for a minute, watching her face. "Neither do I. Why didn't you tell me you knew Bruin?" She nearly fell out of her seat. He might as well have hit her in the chest with a baseball bat.

"I don't know Bruin! Where in the world did you get that idea?" Her face was blushed and beads of sweat appeared on her upper lip.

"Perhaps, he told me." He was fishing again.

"He's lying!"

"Now, why would he do that?"

"I… I don't know."

"Why don't you tell me how you two know each other? It will save a lot of time. I will find out eventually anyway."

She began to cry, feeling the pressure, realizing her world was crashing down around her. "I did a terrible thing. I was mad…and hurt. I'm so sorry," she whined. "He came to see me. Bruin did. A few weeks ago. He said he had heard that there was a certain somebody that had done a bad thing to me. Said he would… fix him… for fifty thousand dollars. I told him I didn't have fifty thousand dollars. Then he said he would do it for ten. I was in love with John. He said he was going to divorce his wife and we would be together. Then, he changed his mind. Said we were through," she sobbed. "I was so hurt. I got the money and gave it to Bruin the next day."

"Did he say how he was going to 'fix him'?"

"No. I think I knew… but he didn't actually say. What's going to happen to me?"

"It's a crime to pay somebody to kill another person. It's the same as doing the killing yourself."

"Oh, God. So, he stole Noah's gun and killed John?"

"No… he didn't do it. Somebody beat him to it. Not that that changes anything as far as you are concerned. You still committed the crime of conspiracy to commit murder."

Her head snapped up. "He didn't do it? Bruin didn't do it?"

"No."

"So, Noah did do it?"

"Well, it does look that way. It'll be up to a jury to decide. In the meantime, you're under arrest for conspiracy to commit murder." He took out the handcuffs. "You have the right to remain silent…"

Chapter 29

Helen Pritchard was near a nervous breakdown. She had called Preston four times in the last fifteen minutes. "He is in a meeting with some of the board members, Mrs. Pritchard. He will call you as soon as it is over," so said his secretary… for the fourth time.

"I'm on the board… why wasn't I informed of this meeting?" she yelled into the phone.

"I'm not sure, Mrs. Pritchard."

She slammed down the phone, went to the liquor cabinet and poured a generous shot of bourbon, downing it in one gulp. It was all over the news. Linda Ross had been arrested for hiring an unnamed assailant to murder her estranged lover… John Pritchard.

"Preston, you son of a bitch! Call me!" she screamed, throwing the glass in the corner, breaking it into a thousand pieces. As if he had been waiting for the request, the phone rang.

"What's wrong?"

"Did you give Bruin our money?" she rasped, barely able to talk.

"Helen, not on the phone! I'll be there in a little while."

"You had better come now. Linda Ross has been arrested. I think we'll be next."

"Shit! Call Orville Merrell. Have him meet us at your place. I'm on the way."

Chapter 30

Sam Gretch turned Linda Ross over to a female officer for the booking process and headed for his desk and the two hours of paperwork waiting for him. Getting her confession was easier than he had thought it would be. A bit of luck, really.

"Captain wants to see you, Sam. Right away," Jimmy Frost informed him.

"Okay," he replied, then headed for his boss' office.

"Get in here and shut the door."

He did as ordered. "What's up?"

"Why are you harassing Preston Broderick?"

"Harassing? That's bull shit! I have reason to believe Broderick and the Pritchard woman paid our missing Bruin to kill her husband... along with Linda Ross!"

"Really? Why haven't you said anything?"

"I wanted to be sure. Now, I'm pretty sure."

"You'd better be. The chief got a call from the mayor... said to get off Broderick's back, now!"

"Did you know the mayor and Bruin are cousins?

"You are shitting me!" Boldery's eyes were as big as walnuts.

"Nope, I'm not."

The captain sat back in his chair. "Wow, do we have our hands full. The mayor and Broderick are as close as two fleas on a dog's ass. Holy shit!"

"Yeah, holy shit is right!"

"So, Noah Ross is innocent? Bruin did it?"

"I didn't say that. I don't think Bruin did it. He was just paid to do it. Somebody beat him to the draw. The evidence still points to Ross, but I still believe he is being framed."

"Wait a minute... go over that again... this is getting complicated."

Orville Merrell was the attorney when the need arose, whom everybody wanted, but only the affluent and very wealthy could afford. People like the mayor of Elmhurst, the president of their largest bank and the like. His fee started at $400 per hour and went up from there. Although his talents were not usually called upon to defend one of his clients in a felony charge, his firm had the manpower and resources to do just that. He was having lunch with a real-estate mogul at Phil Stefani's restaurant on Rush Street when the call came.

"Yes, Helen... yes, of course. Can I call you back? I'm in the middle of lunch." He paused, a concerned look coming over his face. "I see. I'll send Francis over to your house immediately. Don't talk to anyone until he gets there. No one, understand?"

Noah found an empty spot a few yards down the street from Beatrice's office and parked his car. It was their first meeting to start planning his defense. Her office just happened to be in the same block as the bank. Two female bank employees were returning from lunch and had to pass him on the walk. They glanced in his direction, recognized who he was and turned their heads away.

"Good afternoon to you, too!" he said loudly, his feelings hurt.

The two girls quickened their pace.

"I didn't do it!" he yelled after them. Dejected, he walked slowly on down the street.

"Don't let it worry you," Beatrice offered, a few minutes later. "People can be so rude sometimes."

"What happened to innocent until proven guilty?"

"That, my dear Noah, is a myth, I'm afraid!"

"I suppose. Well, where do we start?"

"Did you hear about Linda?"

"Linda? Now what?"

"She's been arrested."

Noah couldn't believe his ears. "For what?"

"Conspiracy to commit murder, so says my source. She apparently hired, or tried to hire, somebody to kill John Pritchard."

"Are you serious?" He was in near shock.

"That's what I'm being told."

"So she knows who did it?"

"Apparently the guy she hired didn't do it. Somebody else did it first."

"Good God! So what does that mean for us?"

"Nothing, right now, I'm afraid. The police think you got there first. It could have a bearing on the case, though. We'll have to wait and see what develops. It might be enough to install reasonable doubt in the mind of the jury. In the meantime, we still need to prepare a defense."

"Yeah… yes, of course."

"Do you know a Shirley Sutkin?"

"No. Who is she?"

"She's the witness who saw you running away from the Pritchard's house."

"She couldn't have."

"I know. I'll destroy her testimony in cross. She never got out of her driveway and that's three blocks from the Pritchard house. Let's talk about the gun. Do you really think Linda had it under the seat of her car?"

"Well, it's possible. Maybe she was planning to kill Pritchard before she hired someone else."

"Could be. Anyway, I plan to play the 'you ain't that dumb' angle. No one would be dumb enough to hide the gun with their fingerprints on it in such a conspicuous place as a mail box... unless they wanted it to be found. We will try to convince the jury that somebody planted it... set you up."

"They did!"

"By the way, how could your fingerprints be the only ones on the gun?"

Noah shrugged. "It was in a holster. I don't know how they could have taken it out without leaving prints. Maybe they didn't take it out. I don't know."

"Okay. Also, it is very important that we establish when you found out about Linda and Pritchard's affair."

"I told you... I didn't know until Sam Gretch told me. Pritchard had been dead for three days."

"Okay, we'll put Gretch on the stand. Let's hope he agrees with you."

Chapter 31

Sam Gretch rang the doorbell and waited. After a few minutes, the door was opened by a man whom he had never seen before.

"May I help you?" There was no hiding the expensive tailor-made suit and the two-hundred dollar tie. *So, Helen Pritchard has brought in the Calvary,* he thought.

"I'm here to see Mrs. Pritchard. I'm Detective Gretch. I have a few questions."

"I'm afraid Mrs. Pritchard is busy, sir."

"Who are you?"

"My name is Francis Pewter. I'm her attorney."

"Well Mr. Peter… I can talk to her here, or I can talk to her down at the station. Which do you think she would prefer?" He had deliberately mispronounced the name.

"Very well. Please come in. My name is not Peter, it is Pewter."

"Yeah, that's what I said… Mr. Peter." Sam followed the suit into the foyer and on into the living room. Here he was greeted by another surprise. Preston Broderick was seated beside Mrs. Pritchard on the sofa.

"Well, look what we have here. Good, you just saved me some time. I really wanted to talk to you both."

"We have nothing to say to you, Detective. I made a call this morning and you will soon be told to quit harassing us!" Broderick offered.

"Oh, I've heard that speech already." Sam waved his hand. "Problem is, we cops just are not smart enough to recognize when we're in big trouble. Also, warnings from higher-ups don't count when the subject is guilty of a serious crime."

"Mr. Gretch, both of these people are clients of the firm of Orville Merrell and Associates and I have instructed them not to answer any of your questions."

"I see. Then perhaps you can explain why they both paid a man named Bruin to murder John Pritchard?"

Helen's hand flew to her mouth and a small moan escaped.

"That's ridiculous!" Broderick stated.

"Is it, now? I already have information about the two of you withdrawing large sums of money a few weeks ago. I have subpoenaed Bruin's bank records and I'm pretty sure I'll find two checks made out by the two of you. I should have the information later this afternoon. Now, what do you think… is it still ridiculous?"

Broderick smiled. "There will be no record of any checks. Not from us."

Sam smiled back. "Yeah, I know. I was just playing with you. Bruin's deposits were made in cash. Funny, though, they were for the same exact amounts that you two withdrew."

"Coincidences happen," the attorney said.

"Yeah, right. You know, conspiring to kill someone is a serious crime. You better hope you have covered all your tracks. I'm a pretty good cop. If I find the slightest crack, I'll be back with an arrest warrant."

"Then we're through here?" Pewter asked.

"For now, Mr. Peter. I'll let myself out. Linda Ross sends her best, by the way."

Chapter 32

Linda Ross, now dressed in the familiar orange of the Cook County Jail residents, was seated at the same table where her husband had been only a short time before. A female police officer was standing just inside the door and Sam Gretch was pacing around the table. They were awaiting the arrival of the court appointed lawyer, a Mr. Horton.

"Is there anything you want to tell me before your attorney gets here?"

"Like what?" She tried to sound brave. Actually, she was terrified.

"Oh, like… who else was in this with you and Bruin. I might be able to offer you a deal… for your testimony against the others."

"I … I don't know any others."

"I think you do. Are you aware of the penalty if you are convicted of conspiracy to commit murder?"

"No."

"Life sentence… with possible parole after 25 years."

"What if he didn't do it?"

"Bruin? Doesn't matter. If there is a conspiracy to commit a crime… that is a crime in itself."

She began to cry. Gretch didn't want her crying when her lawyer got there. "Let's discuss it later. Talk to the public defender. Then we'll talk. I'll be back after he gets here." He left instructions to be called with the female uniform at the door and went to find Jimmy Frost.

Chapter 33

Mayor Philip Augustine was an overweight, ruddy faced man who always had a smile on his face. A born politician if there ever was one. Only today, he wasn't smiling.

"Godammit, Preston!" he yelled into the phone, "what the hell happened? Avery fuck this up? We weren't ready for this yet!"

"Phillip, Bruin didn't do this. We don't know who did."

"Avery didn't do it?"

"No, Phillip, Avery didn't do it."

"Then why in the hell is he running?"

"You'll have to ask him that."

"Well, what about this Ross woman? How did she get messed up in all this?"

"I'm not sure. I suspect Bruin was trying to make a little extra money. Helen and I didn't know John was having an affair with the Ross woman. Bruin must have found out and tried to get her to go in with the plan."

"Good God! You'd better keep me out of this, Preston. You get that high priced asshole Merrell to fix this… now!" The line went dead.

Sam Gretch and Jimmy Frost were having sandwiches and coffee at Garland's Bar.

"Look at it this way, Sam. At least you didn't have a partner very long."

Sam smiled. "That's true. I should be thankful."

"So, what do you think about all this?"

"I still think somebody is setting Noah Ross up. There is more to this than meets the eye. If Helen Pritchard knew her husband was screwing Linda Ross… why didn't she just divorce him? She could have gotten all his money anyway. And Preston Broderick… hiring a hit man? Taking a big chance that he would be named president? It just doesn't make sense. These aren't stupid people!"

"So which one of them killed Pritchard?"

"I don't think any of them did!"

"Well, somebody did. I saw his picture in the paper, under Dead People."

"Funny."

"Did Linda Ross implicate Broderick or Helen Pritchard?"

"No, not yet. If she does, I'll trade her a slap on the hand to testify against them. The conspiracy thing won't be hard to prove. But that ain't going to save Noah Ross."

The two were interrupted by Sam's cell phone.

"Mrs. Ross's attorney is here."

Chapter 34

Bernie Horton looked like a frightened eighteen year old at his first prom. He had been out of law school for only five months. This was his first appointed case. Sam felt a tinge of sympathy. A tinge.

"I have instructed my client not to answer you direct… to let me tell you what it is you want to know," he squeaked.

"Listen, Bernie… may I call you Bernie? This lady paid a cop ten thousand dollars to kill her ex-lover. She's looking at twenty five years. She won't be nearly as pretty after twenty five years of prison life. Now, whatever you do, you keep reminding her of that. I've got a lot of latitude on this. I want to know if she acted alone… or if there were others who, for their own reasons, paid Avery Bruin to kill John Pritchard."

"Yes… there were others. But, she isn't sure who they are."

"What? She doesn't know who they are?" His eyes went to Linda's face. "Mrs. Ross, now is not the time to play games. If you know who they are, tell me. I'll get you out of this mess!"

"He didn't say… names," she whimpered. "He said I knew who they were. I assumed… well, he didn't say names. So I can't say for sure, even though I think I know."

Gretch frowned. He needed names. He needed her to be sure.

"She can't be sure, Detective. Where do we go from here?" Bernie really didn't know where they would go from there.

"Well, I'm afraid she will have to stay put. Unless she can arrange bail money. If I can do this another way, her testimony could possibly still help. We'll have to wait and see." He paused. "Why don't we keep the fact that she doesn't know names a secret? Perhaps I can get the other suspects to slip up… if they think Mrs. Ross knows who they are."

"Couldn't that put her in danger?" Bernie wasn't so dumb.

"Yes, it could. I can put her in protective custody while she's in jail. If she is not in jail, there is not much I can do. She needs to evaluate the risk. She helps me, I help her. Talk to her, Bernie. Call me tomorrow."

Chapter 35

Sam Gretch had a small, but nice, two-bedroom apartment on a quiet street away from the downtown area. It was after eight when he parked the car, walked up the steps and unlocked the door. Inside, he turned on the small hallway light and deposited his gun and shield on the stand by the door. There was light shining under the closed bedroom door.

"You there?" he asked.

"Yeah… I was taking a nap. You woke me up."

"You hungry?"

"I'm starved!"

"Well, get out here. I'll fix us some dinner."

"I'm naked."

"Oh." He considered that. "Okay, I'll come in there. Dinner can wait!"

The alarm went off at 5:30. Sam Gretch hit the snooze button, rolled over and buried his head between her breasts.

"Why do you get up so damned early?" she mumbled.

"I don't usually get up till nine, but today, I thought we could have an early morning romp. What do you say?"

"I bet you ask all the girls that, huh?"

"Nope… just the ones who have law degrees. I'm pretty particular." His lips were teasing her nipples.

"You know I could lose my license… oh, that feels good… if the right people find out about us… oh, don't stop."

"I know. We'll be careful." His lips moved lower.

"My god! Who gives a shit about a law license?"

Later, they had showered, dressed and were having coffee at the kitchen table.

"I was serious about losing my license."

"I know you were, Beatrice. Perhaps we should stop seeing each other until this thing with Noah Ross is over."

"I don't want to… but I think we should."

He kissed her on the forehead. "I'll miss you. See you soon."

Chapter 36

He arrived at the police station at 7:15 and attacked the stack of paper work he had left the day before. Around 8:30 the desk sergeant walked by and tossed an envelope on his desk.

"Somebody left this for you, Sam. I didn't see who it was."

"Thanks, Gene." He lay it aside and finished the report, then tore open the envelope. There was a single sheet of paper with several sentences typed, double spaced.

DO YOU LIKE SPORTS?

WOULD YOU LIKE SPORTS TO BE CLOSER?

DO YOU HAVE 46 ACRES FOR A NEW STADIUM?

WOULD YOU KILL TO GET WHAT YOU WANT?

IF YOU CAN ANSWER YES TO ALL THE ABOVE, YOU JUST MIGHT BE GUILTY OF SOMETHING.

Carefully, he replaced the paper in the envelope and called the Cook County Crime Lab.

"Gary, I have a sheet of paper I want you to check out… see if there are any prints or anything that could help me figure out where it came from."

Chapter 37

The trial was not going well. Gordon Sterns was relentless in pointing out at every opportunity that the murder weapon did in fact belong to the defendant and that his prints were the only ones on it. Also, Mrs. Sutkin, although admitting during cross that she didn't actually see Noah at the Pritchard residence, did establish that he was definitely in the area on the morning of the murder. It seemed to Noah that the jury was nodding their heads at every statement Sterns made.

"Don't give up yet, I have a few things up my sleeve as well," Beatrice tried to reassure him. He had noticed that Robbie was sitting directly behind the defendant's table. *At least he doesn't have to worry about missing work*, Noah thought bitterly

It was only the third day and the prosecution had already called their last witness.

"We have motive, we have established that Mr. Ross was in the area and had opportunity, and most importantly, we have the murder weapon. The prosecution rests, Your Honor." Gordon Sterns sat, unable to hide the smug smile playing around the corners of his lips. It was now up to the defense.

"The defense would like to call Detective Sam Gretch." Beatrice announced.

A murmur went through the court room. Arresting officers were usually part of the prosecution. Sterns was up quickly.

"I object, Your Honor!"

"On what grounds, Mr. Sterns?" At this point, Judge Lillian Gray was inclined to give the defense as much help as she could. Although the hard evidence was overwhelming, she still wasn't convinced this man could commit cold-blooded murder.

"Detective Gretch was the arresting officer. He is listed on the prosecutions list of possible witnesses."

"Then take him off, Mr. Sterns. I will allow him to testify for the defense. If he is on your list, his testimony should be to your advantage."

Sam was sworn in and took the stand. He tried to avoid eye contact with Beatrice, but was not sure why. Perhaps he feared that somebody would jump up and yell 'Foul! They've been sleeping together." But nobody did.

"Detective Gretch, the prosecution has stated that Mr. Ross murdered John Pritchard because the deceased was having an affair with his wife. Thus, they have claimed to have established motive. But in fact, was it not you who informed Mr. Ross of that fact… three days after the murder?"

"Yes."

"In your opinion, was this the first that Mr. Ross had heard about his wife having an affair?"

"Yes."

"I object!" Sterns interrupted.

"Your Honor, Detective Gretch was the only person present during this conversation. I have the right to ask his opinion."

"I agree. Overruled. You may continue."

"Was Noah Ross cooperative in this investigation?"

"Yes, very cooperative."

"And, why do you think that is?"

"We object, Your Honor!" Sterns came out of his chair.

"Mr. Sterns, I have already ruled that Detective Gretch's opinions will be allowed during this testimony, as long as the jury knows these are just his opinions. Please refrain from making similar objections!"

"Yes, Your Honor," he said, giving up.

"I'll repeat the question. Why do you think Mr. Ross was so cooperative during your investigation, Detective?" Beatrice continued.

Sam paused, thinking carefully about that. "I don't think he had anything to hide. I think at the time he thought his brother might have committed the crime. He was very interested in proving that that was not the case."

"At that point, did you think the murderer could be Robbie Ross, the defendant's brother?"

"Yes… he was considered a suspect."

"But not later."

"No. He had an alibi. He was in Minnesota at the time."

"What about the gun, Detective Gretch. Are you positive it was the murder weapon?"

"Yes, without a doubt."

"Did you think it strange that the gun was found so easily?"

"Yes. But, the killer may have not been thinking straight. Criminals have been known to have made worse mistakes."

"Was the gun in a holster when it was found?"

"No… just the gun."

"The forensic report said there were traces of fabric and plastic found on the gun which is normally found in a holster, is that correct?"

"Yes, that is correct."

"So, it would seem that the gun was stored in a holster at some point?"

"Yes."

"I would like to call the court's attention to exhibit seventeen; an identical holster to the one Mr. Ross, and others, have stated was on the gun when it was in the safe." Beatrice brought the holster to the stand. "If a gun stored in this holster was not removed, would the finger prints of the previous handler remain on the weapon?"

"Yes."

"So, if Mr. Ross fired his weapon, at a firing range, say, and replaced it in the holster, his prints would remain on the gun."

"Yes."

"Detective Gretch, would it be possible to fire a gun in this holster without removing it?" Another murmur went through the room.

Sam paused, looking at the holster. It was made from thin plastic, covered by a canvas fabric. There was a hole in the bottom at the end of the barrel portion. "That would be doubtful. There is no way to pull the trigger."

"Is that the only reason? Would the bullet be interfered with?"

"No, the bullet would exit okay. There is no obstruction for the bullet."

"So, if one could find a way to pull the trigger, a gun could be fired by a person other than the owner of the fingerprints."

"Yes, but I don't see how that could be done."

"Your Honor, I would like to introduce a visual aid. It has bearing on this case to illustrate to the court how this could have been done."

Sterns knew better than to object. Beatrice went to the defense table and returned with a small sack.

From it, she removed what appeared to be an exact replica of the holster. She handed it to detective Gretch.

He examined it and couldn't help but smile.

"Detective Gretch, please tell the court about this holster."

"It is identical to the other one, except it has had a hole cut in the side that gives one access to the trigger." He held it up for the jury and then the judge to see. A murmur went through the court room.

"So, a gun in this holster, could be fired without being removed?"

"Yes."

"I cut that out with a pair of office scissors," Beatrice announced. "Now, Detective Gretch, I have only a few more questions." She paused for effect. "It is clear that the evidence in this case suggests that Mr. Ross is guilty, do you agree?"

"Yes."

"And evidence is rarely wrong, do you agree?

"Yes."

"But sometimes, it can be wrong… do you agree with that?

"Yes, sometimes."

She paused, letting the tension build, for nearly an entire minute. "In your opinion, detective Gretch, did Noah Ross kill John Pritchard?"

The court room was so quiet; one could have heard a fish fart from the bottom of a fifty gallon tank. Gretch looked to the judge and then to the jury… and finally at Noah Ross.

"No, I don't believe he did." The court room erupted.

Chapter 38

"Are you out of your mind? What the hell is wrong with you?" Boldery yelled.

"I just told the truth. You want me to lie on the stand?"

"Well, you didn't have to tell the truth quite so damned convincingly!" The two were in Boldery's office. The door was closed but that didn't keep the rest of the squad from hearing Sam get his ass chewed out.

"Glad I'm not in there," Jimmy Frost remarked. "The old man is really pissed."

"He'll get over it. Sam always lands on his feet," a fellow cop commented.

Sam was silent for a few minutes, letting Boldery vent his anger. "Okay, calm down and listen to me. There is something very big going on. I'm not sure that it relates to the Ross case, but I'm sure it relates to John Pritchard's murder. I think Noah Ross accidentally got caught up in it, somehow."

"What do you mean?"

"Well, I'm pretty sure that Bruin was hired to kill John Pritchard by his wife and Broderick. Somebody got there first and is trying to frame Noah Ross. I think that has messed up Broderick's original plans, although I don't know how just yet. Noah Ross is probably going to be convicted, and that's a shame. But when I find out the whole story, maybe I can put the real killer in jail and let Noah Ross free.

There has got to be a reason that Broderick and the Pritchard woman wanted Pritchard out of the way. I don't think it was so Broderick could be bank president, and I don't think it was because Pritchard was screwing Linda Ross. It's much bigger than that. I've got a new lead to follow up on, and I got a feeling we are going to be battling City Hall on this one. Broderick and the mayor are very close and somebody with pull had to get Bruin here in the first place. It's going to get rough, boss. Don't you bail out on me."

"I knew it! Sam Gretch, you are going to get me killed!"

"Just stay clean, boss. They might try to bring you on board. Just stay clean."

Chapter 39

Gordon Sterns gave an outstanding summation to the jury. Even Noah was nearly convinced he had killed John Pritchard.

"Of course, sometimes evidence is wrong… but not in this case. Of course, someone could have cut a hole in the holster and fired Noah Ross' gun. Of course we all hate to see a good citizen commit an act of violence. Mr. Ross' attorney did a good job of confusing you with what could have happened. But there were no facts in any of that. Just opinions. Facts verses opinions. That's what we have here. But you must deal only with the facts. Mr. Ross's gun was the murder weapon. Fact. Mr. Ross' fingerprints were the only ones on the gun. Fact. Mr. Ross was seen three blocks from the murder within minutes of the crime. Fact. Mr. Ross' wife was having an affair with the deceased. Fact. Those are the facts. That is what you must base your decision on. Facts."

There was no room in the court room for any additional people. Even the standing area at the back of the room was full.

"You did a good job, Beatrice," Noah whispered. "You didn't have much to work with. At least I bet you made them think a bit. I thank you for that." Noah smiled a tired smile. "You will come and visit me once in awhile, won't you?"

She smiled in return. "I know it's bad, Noah. We didn't have enough ammo to fight with. But, don't give up. Someday, we'll know the truth, and someday… we will get you out. I'll promise you that." She had resigned herself to the fact that she would loose this case.

They were interrupted by the jury room door opening and the twelve jurors filing in. The judge entered a few seconds later.

"All rise," so ordered the bailiff. "This court is in session. The Honorable Judge Lillian Gray presiding."

"Jurors, have you reached a verdict?"

"We have, Your Honor." The bailiff took the written verdict to the judge, who read it with care. "Will the defendant please stand."

Noah stood on shaky legs. Beatrice stood at his side.

"How say you?"

"We find the defendant, Noah Ross, guilty of first degree murder."

Noah fell into his chair and covered his face with his hands. He had been expecting it, but it was still devastating to actually hear it.

"Thank you, Madam Foreman. Members of the jury, you are dismissed. Thank you for your service. Mr. Ross, you have been found guilty by a jury of your peers. Sentencing will be in three weeks. You will be remanded into the Cook County Holding Facility until sentencing. That is all. This court is adjourned!"

"Can I buy you a drink, counselor?"

"Thanks, Sam. I can sure as hell use one." The two of them were walking down the steps of the court house.

"Is it safe for us to be seen together now?"

"Sure. We are no longer involved in the same case. I can date anyone I choose."

"Date? Who said anything about a date? I just want to get laid!" he joked.

"That may never happen again, fella! At least, not until after you buy me a drink, followed by a nice dinner."

The two linked arms and walked toward Garland's Bar. Even though she had been prepared to lose, it was never easy to lose.

"What do we do now?"she asked.

"Figure out who really killed John Pritchard and get Noah out of prison."

"That may take some time."

"It doesn't matter how long it takes. I won't stop trying."

Chapter 40

The phone rang. It was Gary from the lab.

"I got nothing from the note, Sam. Same thing for the envelope. It was clean as a whistle except for your prints. Sorry."

"Okay, Gary. Thanks. Send it back to me." He opened his desk drawer and read the copy he had made of the note.

DO YOU LIKE SPORTS?

WOULD YOU LIKE SPORTS TO BE CLOSER?

DO YOU HAVE 46 ACRES FOR A NEW STADIUM?

WOULD YOU KILL TO GET WHAT YOU WANT?

IF YOU CAN ANSWER YES TO ALL THE ABOVE, YOU JUST MIGHT BE GUILTY OF SOMETHING.

Somebody knows what is going on, other than the bad guys. Who ever that is wants me to know also. Why don't they just tell me? He leaned back in his chair and closed his eyes. *Because, they're part of the plan... perhaps reluctantly. Because they want it stopped, but they don't want to get in trouble. Or maybe, they're just fucking with me. Now who could that be?*

He left the station and drove over to the Cook County Holding Facility.

"I'd like to see Linda Ross, please." He showed the officer his I.D.

"Of course, detective. Have a seat in room 8. I'll bring her in there."

He did as he was told and a few minutes later, the door opened and a very tired looking Linda Ross entered, followed by the officer.

"You want me to stay, sir?" he asked.

"No, that won't be necessary. I can run faster than she can," Sam joked.

After the officer left, Sam pulled out a chair from the table. "Sit down, Linda," he offered. "Are you alright?"

"I shouldn't be talking to you without my lawyer."

"I'm not here to discuss your case. Not today. However, any help you can give me will not be forgotten… when it does come time to talk about your case."

"Okay. It's not too bad… in the protected area. I'm in a cell by myself and nobody bothers me. What do you want from me? You sure I don't need my lawyer today?"

"Who has fifty acres in town that would house a sports stadium?" He decided to be direct.

Her eyes shot up and she couldn't hide the surprise registered on her face. "Why would you ask me that?"

"You're a real-estate agent. Who better?"

She was still for a moment. "The walls are about to start crumbling down, aren't they?" she said softly.

"I don't know. You tell me." He knew he had hit pay dirt.

"There's a forty six acre parcel of farm land that used to belong to the Diehl family on the west edge of town. A few years back, the Elmhurst State Bank purchased it... a transaction handled by John Pritchard. I was not personally in on the sale, but my firm handled the details. That's when I met John. He wanted to make a city park out of it... big fountain, picnic area, play grounds, little league ball park... all that stuff."

"So the purchase was public knowledge?"

"Yes, as far as I know. But John couldn't get the board to agree to donate the land to the Park District. I think he said it was a five to two vote. Even his wife voted no."

"Who was the other no vote?"

"Some guy named Frost. I never met him."

"Doesn't majority rule?"

"No, not in financial matters involving over a million dollars. The bank's bylaws state the board has to be unanimous."

"So what did the others want to do with the property?"

"I thought you knew that already. Didn't you mention a sports stadium?"

"For who?"

"Professional football... a dome."

Sam let that sink in. "Wow. We're talking about a lot of money. Replacing Soldier Field."

"Yes, a lot of money," Linda agreed.

"You realize you have just given me the names I wanted without actually giving me names?"

"I don't know for sure if they were the others who hired Bruin. He never said they were."

"He didn't have to. Well, at least now, I know why Broderick and Helen Pritchard wanted John Pritchard out of the way. Now, I have to prove they were part of the conspiracy to have him killed. Thank you, Linda Ross. I'm sorry you're in here. But, you did commit a serious crime. When the danger is past, I'll set you free. You have my word on it."

Sam headed back toward Elmhurst and drove straight to the bank. He approached a teller and asked her if she had a bank brochure that listed the board of directors.

"Oh, yes, sir. On the table just to the right of the entry doors."

Back in the car, he read the list with care. The brochure had not been reprinted since the death of John Pritchard and still listed him as Bank President. The list included:

John Pritchard
Helen Pritchard
Preston Broderick
Orville Merrell
Donald Augustine
Willard Diehl
Arthur Frost

So the bank purchased property from one of the board members, Willard Diehl, approved by the infamous Orville Merrell along with the town mayor, Donald Augustine. No problem getting the approval to purchase. Now, what to do with the property? A park, which made neither the bank nor its board members any money... or a sports dome, which would make everybody tons of money. Duh! Only, John Pritchard said no. And, so did Arthur Frost. John Pritchard is dead. Now, who is Arthur Frost?

Chapter 41

Menard State Prison is a Level 1, maximum security facility for adult males. It is not a pretty facility. It is not a comfortable facility. It is ugly, it is hard and it was now the home to Mr. Noah Ross… for the next thirty years or so.

They shaved his head. No explanation was given for that. They stuck a gloved finger up his ass. That, he knew why they did. He carried a sheet, a blanket, a small pillow and a roll of toilet paper as he followed the uniformed guard down the cell lined hallway. The welcome committee was present.

"Hey, Brutus… we got new meat!"

"Yeah, I see! Cute butt, huh?"

"Not bad! I'm gettin' hard!"

"Yank it off, idiot. Nobody wants your little hard on!"

"That you, Rufus? If it is… get fucked!"

Noah's knees were trembling, causing him to walk unsteady. The guard was a tall and muscular black man.

"I'm Andy. Don't let 'em scare ya, man! If they see you're afraid, they won't let up. The guy next to you is a good guy. Stay next to him… and learn."

"Thanks. This ain't going to be fun, is it?"

The guard laughed. "Fun? No, I think not."

Then they were there. Cell number 446. Home sweet home. The door slammed.

"Good luck, man. Breakfast is at seven, lunch is at twelve and dinner is at six. They'll let you know when it's time to exercise and take showers and stuff like that." The guard was gone.

He made his bed and surveyed the room. The walls were gray. Of course they would be gray. Silhouettes of past posters and remnants of old tape were the only decorations. One small table about two feet square, a straight back chair, an empty shelf over the table and a lidless, stainless steel toilet stool which was now accompanied by a roll of thin paper. *How in the hell will I ever be able to do this?*

"Howdy neighbor." The voice came from the next cell. It reminded Noah of Wilson, Tim Allen's faceless neighbor on Tool Time. Any other time it would have made him laugh. Not today.

"Hi." It was all he could muster.

"My name is Harley. What's yours?"

"Noah."

"Noah? Like in the Bible Noah?"

"Yeah... just like in the Bible."

"The last man in your cell died."

"From what?"

"A screw driver in the eye."

Noah shook his head in disbelief. "What did he do?"

"Ran into a screw driver, I guess. I never asked."

"Why are you telling me this?"

"So that you know... you should never ask. And, watch out for screwdrivers."

"I see. Any other advice?"

There was a pause. "Always stay next to someone you trust... share your food if somebody wants it... say sir to the guards... and keep your nose out of where it don't belong. All easy stuff."

"Yeah, sounds like easy stuff. A walk in the park, huh?"

The man giggled. "I like you Noah. Would you like to join me for dinner?"

Chapter 42

At six o'clock exactly, a horn sounded and all the cell doors opened at once. Noah stood, but hesitated to go out of the cell. He felt immense fear. At least in his cell he was safe… from things. Prisoners were rushing past, paying no attention to him. *Feeding time at the zoo*, he thought.

"Are you ready for dinner, Noah of the Bible?" The man was thin, with pure white hair. Noah was shocked at his age. He had to be in his late eighties. "I'm Harley. Let's go eat." He reached out a frail looking hand for Noah to shake. It was surprisingly firm. "Let me officially welcome you to Menard."

They followed the crowd down two different hallways and entered the mess hall. The food line moved fast and soon they were seated at one of the metal tables. His plate contained two pork chops, a scoop of green beans, a scoop of mashed potatoes and a slice of bread. Tentatively, he took a small bite, finding that it was actually quite good. Then, a little surprised that he was hungry, he attacked his food which quickly disappeared.

"Next time, leave one of the chops… in case one of the Gangers wants it," Harley whispered.

"Really? Ganger? In here?"

"Most assuredly, in here. We have several different gangs."

"So, save some of my food… for them?

"A small price to pay for peace, wouldn't you agree?"

"Yes. Yes, that is a small price to pay. I have a lot to learn."

"I am here to teach."

"How long have you been here?"

"Twenty two years, five months and eleven days."

Their conversation was interrupted by a huge man, every inch of his arms from his wrists to his shoulders covered in tattoos, as he sat across from them.

"New student, Harley?" His voice was deep and his face was scared from many battles.

"Yes, first day, Mr. General."

"What ya in fer?"

"Murder." Noah answered. *Murder. I was convicted of murder.*

The man pursed his lips and nodded. "Innocent?"

"Yes." *Of course I'm innocent!*

Mr. General lifted his head and roared in laughter. "Hey guys… we got a murderer here… and he's innocent!" he yelled at the top of his voice.

"Me too!"

"Yeah, I didn't do nothin'!"

"Me either! Let me out!"

"Call the newspaper… stop the presses!"

The hoots and howls lasted at least two minutes. Noah actually smiled. "Not too sympathetic, I guess." To which the General roared again, slapping Noah on the shoulder.

"Shit and syphilis, that's where you find sympathy… in between… in the dictionary. Sure as hell won't find any here in this Goddamn place! You goin' to eat that bread?"

"You're welcome to it, sir."

"Well thank you, little man. You're a gentleman." He picked up the bread and crushed it between his large fingers, forming it into a little round ball, and then dropped it back on Noah's plate.

"That was delightful. See you around." The huge man rose and walked away as the horn sounded again. Dinner was over.

Noah didn't sleep at all the first night. There was no way. So many things on his mind. How did he ever end in up in a place like this. Just trying to make a living… wanting so bad to do that by writing books. And Linda… losing her so quickly… and so easily. *Thank God we never had children.* He remembered wondering once a long time ago if men in prison undressed at night. Well, this one didn't. At six a.m. the horn sounded and some of the cell doors slammed open. His remained shut. Harley stuck his head around the corner.

"Shower and shave. Odd numbers today. Even numbers tomorrow. Be back for breakfast."

Noah was not looking forward to going to the showers; especially after he found out he would not be going with Harley. Even though Harley was old and weak, he felt safe when they were together.

"What should I do in the showers to stay safe?" he asked, after they had filled their breakfast trays and sat at the same table as yesterday.

"Stay next to the General. He's ugly, but I think he likes you, and he's straight. He has an even numbered cell as well."

Noah wasn't convinced. "How do you know he likes me?"

"Well, he didn't spit on you… nor did he physically harm you. A good first impression, I'd say…based on past experiences."

"I see." He really didn't. "How can I get a computer in here?"

"A computer? We're not allowed access to the internet."

"No, I need it as a word processor… so I can write."

"You're an author?"

"No, I'm a writer. You're not an author unless you have been published."

Harley smiled. "You'll have to let me read some of your work. I'm an avid reader and a pretty good judge of what is good and what is trash."

"So far, all I have is a lot of rejections from publishers."

Harvey nodded. "Your lawyer will have to petition for a computer. If you don't cause any trouble, you can probably get one in a month or so."

"That long?"

"A month is not a long time, Like In the Bible Noah. Not in here."

Chapter 43

On Friday afternoon, Noah Ross received his first visitor. Two guards escorted him to the visitation area, handcuffing him to a waist-chain before he was ushered into the room. His visitor was Robbie.

"Jesus Christ, they always chain you up like that?" Robbie asked, disgustedly.

"I guess. This is my first time."

"Well, it ain't right."

"I'm a convicted murderer, remember?"

"Well, we both know better than that," Robbie snorted.

"No, brother… *that* is a fact. I am a *convicted* murderer. Just because I didn't do it, doesn't mean I wasn't convicted."

Robbie let that sink in. "You doin' okay? I mean, as good as you can?"

"I'm doing okay… so far. The food is decent and no body has bothered me. You talked to Beatrice or Sam?"

"No, I haven't seen either of them. Did you need me to?"

Noah shook his head. "No, I suppose not. It's only been a week. Can't expect them to do anything this quick. My God, Robbie… I still can't believe this happened!"

"We'll get you out, Noah. I'll see to that."

"Sure, little brother. Sure." Noah smiled. *You actually believe that, don't you, son?* "Have you seen Linda?"

Robbie hesitated. “You didn’t know? She was arrested.”

“Arrested! For what?”

“Conspiracy. I guess she paid some guy to kill Pritchard.”

“You are shitting me! Who did she pay… and why ain’t he in here instead of me?”

“I guess she paid him, but he didn’t do it. Anyway, the paper said it was a crime even if the guy didn’t do it.”

Noah starred at the restraints on his hands. “How can a person’s world be completely destroyed so easily?” he mumbled.

“Time’s up!” the guard called.

Chapter 44

Sam had thought about it long and hard before finally picking up the phone and dialing the number of the bank.

"Elmhurst State Bank. How may I help you?"

"Hi, this is John Roberts," he lied. "I'm with the State Banking Regulation Office. We're updating our files on the board members addresses of the Elmhurst bank. We have two members we are not sure of... A Mr. Preston Broderick and a Mr. Arthur Frost. We show Mr. Broderick at 1120 Monroe Ave. in Elmhurst, is that correct?"

"Just a moment, Mr. Roberts, and I'll look." There was a pause. "Yes, sir, that is correct."

"Great. Okay. And, we are showing Mr. Frost at 903 Adams in Joliet."

"Oh, no, sir. That is incorrect. Mr. Frost lives at 556 Church St. in Naperville."

"Really! That's probably why all our correspondence has been returned."

"Yes, sir. I'm sure it is."

"Well, okay... thank you very much."

Naperville was one of those communities that got caught up in the up-scale housing boom in the eighties. It was close enough to the city for an easy commute and was surrounded by several large shopping malls and exclusive restaurants. The community grew at a amazing pace. It was Sam's home town... but it wasn't even close to the one he remembered.

The house was large. Two-story brick and stone, spread over the three acre plot like a giant octopus. Must be ten thousand square feet, he mused. The sun was warm on his back as he walked up the steps, enjoying the smell of the lilacs. He thought about the two bedroom house he grew up in. Long gone, tore down to allow for homes like this. *This baby probably cost over a million*, he surmised.

Ringing the doorbell produced nothing. He had the unexplainable feeling that there was no one in the house… and that there had been no one in the house for some time. He walked around back. The huge cobble stoned patio was covered with a screen enclosure and the large pool inside was covered with a blue tarp. Expensive outdoor furniture, wall decorations and a large wet bar gave proof that these people did not have to worry where their next meal was coming from.

"Wow, what a place. So this is how the other half lives!" Sam muttered out loud. As he was walking back to the front, a neighbor stuck his head over the hedge.

"You have business over there mister? I have my phone in my hand ready to call the police!"

"I am the police, sir." Sam held up his shield and approached the neighbor.

"Is there something wrong officer?"

"No, I just have an important paper for Mr. Frost to sign… from the bank."

"Well, that may be difficult. The Frosts are traveling somewhere in Europe. Been gone a month or so. I'm not sure when they plan to return. I kind of keep an eye on the place. Lots of criminals around, you know?"

Sam smiled. "Yeah, I know. No idea how to get in touch with them, huh?"

"Well, they have a son. He's a policeman... like yourself. Works in one of the western subs. Not sure which one. Maybe he could tell you."

"Yeah, I bet he can. Thank you, sir. I'll be going now." He walked back to the drive, got in his car and headed back to Elmhurst.

I'll be damned! Now I know where the envelope came from. He broke into a grin.

Chapter 45

It was after seven when he got back in town and he headed straight for Garland's Bar.

"Sam! Where you been keepin' yourself? Ain't seen you for a week."

"Just been busy, Jake. Beer, please."

'Sure thing, Here you go," He sat the dripping glass on the bar.

"Jimmy Frost been in tonight?"

"No, not tonight. Ain't seen him."

Sam took out his phone and called Beatrice.

"Where you been all day, Sammie?" Her voice made him smile.

"Had some things to check on. I'm at Garland's. Want to come join me?"

"Be there in twenty minutes."

That thought made him even happier. For some reason, he wanted to have her around tonight.

They had burgers and a few beers, sitting in the most secluded booth at the back, side by side, quietly getting drunk. Jake had joked he would have to put a reserved sign on the table, since the two spent so much time there.

"I wonder how Noah Ross is doing." Beatrice said, out of the blue.

"Yeah, I've been thinking about him too."

She let out a little burp. "Excuse me. That feels better. There was more room for that out there, than in here." She said, pointing at her tummy. "Classy ladies are not supposed to belch, are they?"

"You are one classy lady!" Sam smiled, shaking his head. "Belch all you want!"

"Damned right!" She paused for a minute, studying the bubbles in her beer. "You just never know, do you? You can be walking down the street and wham… a 747 airplane falls on your ass. You didn't cause it. You didn't even know this fucking airplane existed before. It just picks your ass to fall on."

"Sad… but true," Sam added, agreeing with this bit of philosophy. "You know, it just don't add up. I keep finding piles of shit everywhere around this bank… but Noah Ross just doesn't fit in! What am I missing?"

"I don't know, Sammie." She paused. "Is it possible that who ever killed John Pritchard had no knowledge of what was going on at the bank?"

"You mean… like an airplane… just falling from the sky." He was silent for a minute. "Anything is possible. Where have I heard that before?"

She giggled. "I'm horny, Sammie. Let's go home."

"Yours or mine?"

"Which is closer?"

"Yours."

"Then we're going to mine. I'm really horny!"

That proved to be very true. Sometime after two a.m. and three encounters, he begged for mercy and they fell asleep in each other's arms.

Chapter 46

Sam arrived at the station at 7:05 the next morning to find Jimmy Frost sitting beside his desk.

"Been looking for you," Sam informed him.

"So I've heard. Why do you think I'm here?"

"You were at Garland's after me?"

"Yes, and the answers are… yes… I didn't think it mattered at the time… and yes."

"Yes, Arthur Frost is your father. You didn't say anything because you didn't think it was relevant during the Pritchard murder investigation… and the third yes?"

"I told them to go somewhere safe… get out of town for awhile… after Dad told me about the forty seven acres and about how he and John Pritchard were the only two nay votes. And then, John Pritchard was killed."

"You sent the note."

"Yeah… it was a test…for fun." He grinned. "You did good!"

Sam smiled in return. "Couldn't you just tell me."

"Oh, no! What fun would be in that?"

"Anything else you know?"

Jimmy looked around for anyone listening. There was no one. "Well, according to Dad, the mayor has really been pushing for this stadium. After all, it would mean billions in revenue for the town, not to mention the bank. I think I would add him to your suspected list of conspirators."

"Yeah, I already have. Avery Bruin is his second cousin."

"Oh, I didn't know that! Even more reason."

"You should talk to Mulvaney more often."

After Jimmy left, Sam went in to see Captain Boldery. "Can I buy you a cup of coffee… at the diner? I need to talk without the threat of being overheard."

"Sure. Let's go."

They were seated a secluded booth at the rear of the diner, a block from the police station. "Okay, Sam, what's up?" Boldery asked, as soon as the coffee was delivered.

"I want to talk about conspiracy to commit murder."

"I thought that would be the subject."

"Without Bruin, I'm not sure I can prove anything… although I do have Linda Ross. I know Broderick and Helen Pritchard paid Bruin to kill Pritchard, but I can't prove that. I know the mayor was in on it too, but I can't prove that either. Linda Ross, I don't have to prove, she confessed. But her reason for wanting John Pritchard killed was quite different than the others. I'm not sure where to go from here."

"Well, if you're right about the mayor, and I suspect you are, we have to be very careful, and we will have to prove conspiracy without a doubt. Every thing you have so far is circumstantial. That's not going to cut it in this case. Orville Merrell is one of the best. He won't be like some court-appointed lawyer!"

"I agree. So, what do I do?"

"Nothing… now. Wait and watch. Look for Bruin. And look for the real killer of John Pritchard, if you're still so sure Ross is innocent. That should keep you busy."

"Okay, boss. I'll keep you informed."

Chapter 47

One Month Later

"Ross, you got visitors. Let's go." The two guards opened the cell door and put the waist-chain and handcuffs in place.

"Who's here?"

"I am not your social secretary, scumbag. I don't have clue," mumbled one of the guards. Noah remained quiet for the remainder of the walk. Some of the guards were nice, some were not. One learned to respond accordingly.

When they let him in the visitor's room, he was surprised to find his lawyer… and the cop who had arrested him.

"Well, I'll be damned. Detective Gretch. Beatrice has to come… part of my appeal… but I must admit… I didn't expect to see you."

"Hi, Noah… you doing okay?"

"Sure. Nothing a hacksaw and a plane ticket to Jamaica wouldn't fix."

Sam nodded sympathetically. "Listen, I'll leave you two alone. I just wanted to see with my own eyes that you were okay. Here, this is for you." He put a box on the table and left.

"Don't be too hard on him, Noah. He did everything he could for you at your trial."

"Yeah, I know. It's not his fault that I'm in here. It's hard not to be bitter, though. What's in the box?"

Beatrice smiled. "A computer… with the latest word processing software installed. Sam bought it for you. You have been approved by the warden to have it."

"Really? Gretch bought this for me?"

"Yes, he did."

"Wow. I should have been nicer. Please, tell him thanks… thanks very much. And tell him I'm sorry for being such an ass."

"I will."

"Anything new… about my situation?"

"No, I'm afraid not. I know that Sam is working on it, though … every day. Trying to find who really did it."

"Yeah. And I pray… every day… that he finds him."

"Well, we just came to give you the computer. I can't stay. I have to be going." She stood. "I'll see you in a couple of weeks. Enjoy your new toy."

Noah grinned. "You know I will!"

"What have you got there, young man?" Harley inquired, seeing Noah with the box.

"A piece of my life I thought might be gone. I have a computer. I can write again."

"Good for you! You will let me read your essays… once in awhile? I love to read."

"So you said. Sure, Harley. You any good at proof-reading?"

"I think that anybody who doesn't know at least three ways to spell a word is pretty damned dumb! Some words, I can spell four different ways!"

Noah smiled. "Thank God for spell check!"

Chapter 48

Elmhurst City Hall

"Mayor, a collect call from a Mr. Avery for you on line two," his secretary interrupted. Phillip Augustine was standing in the reception area talking to one of his city supervisors.

"Mr. Avery?" For a moment he didn't realize she was talking about his cousin. "Oh, yes… Mr. Avery. I'll take it in my office, Angie. Thanks."

He quickly dismissed the supervisor and nearly ran into his office, slamming the door on the way. "Yes, I'll accept the charges… Avery? That you?"

"I need some money, cuz. You got any layin' around?"

"Where in the hell are you?"

"We'll discuss that later. Right now, I need some money. The ninety-thousand won't last for ever."

"Why did you run?"

"Sam Gretch ain't no dummy. He's already figured out it was probably you who got me hired there in the first place. You want me trying to explain that to a jury?"

"No, I guess not. So, if it wasn't you, who in the hell killed John?"

"I don't have a clue… but who ever it was, they sure fucked things up for us!"

"Yes, well… that's for sure."

"What are you guys going to do now… about the stadium?"

"We can't do anything… not for a long time. It would look too suspicious. Maybe in a couple of years. We'll have to see."

"What about my money."

"Avery, I can't afford to keep you forever."

"Really? Huh. What choice do you have?"

The mayor was quiet for several seconds. "I guess, none."

"You're right, cuz! Call this number at 7:30 p.m. your time tonight; 011-54-11-374-1106. Ask for Rangell. She will give you instructions on how to have the money transferred to my account. Two hundred thou should last me a year or so."

"Where are you?"

"Nice doing business with you, cuz. I'll talk to you next year. Bye."

The mayor slowly hung up the receiver, trying to figure out what to do next. Deciding that he didn't know what to do next, he made another call.

"Merrell and Associates."

"This is Phillip Augustine. I need to talk to Orville."

Bruin locked the door on his meager hotel room and headed for the elevator. Sometimes, it worked… some times it didn't. Nobody seemed to know why. This time it worked and the car rattled into action, descending the nine floors to the lobby.

Hotel De La Paix was not the Ritz Carlton. It was not even the Holiday Inn. In fact, it was not even Motel 6. Located in the heart of Buenos Aries, in an area where no one asked questions, it was a perfect place to wait for his money to arrive. Then, he would upgrade.

The desk clerk was asleep, his feet up on a file cabinet. He was dressed in his usual dirty undershirt and his open mouth displayed several missing teeth.

"Hey, shithead! Wake up."

He nearly fell over backward. "Yes, senor?"

"I'm going out. If my girlfriend comes here, tell her I'll see her around six tonight."

"Oh, yes, senor! I tell her. I tell her very good."

The hotel was only a few blocks from the Banque of the Americanos. He had watched people coming and going for a week, from the sidewalk café across the street. It was not hard to figure which ones were the employees.

He had followed her down a side street into another restaurant and introduced himself as the great American adventurer. Intrigued by his boldness, she allowed herself the pleasure of talking to a man. It was not her usual style. Rangell Alveros became overwhelmed. She was a plain woman, not accustomed to the attraction of good-looking men, especially one from America. She allowed this man to seduce her. Only after several sessions of passionate sex in his small and unkempt hotel room, did he ask for her help. He needed to get a large sum of money transferred… without drawing attention to himself. Then he could rent a better place and show her a much better time. Not a problem… she would be glad to help.

Orville Merrell called Phillip Augustine back at twelve-thirty that afternoon.

"The number is in Buenos Aries, Argentina, Phillip. Probably an international bank. You had better go ahead and make the call and do as instructed. It will take some time to get somebody in place to find him. I'm not even sure I can."

"Okay, Orville. I'll go ahead with it. Like Avery said, what choice do I have?"

"I just can't believe our bad luck on this. Why did somebody have to kill John before we were ready? What are the chances of that?"

Chapter 49

When Sam returned from lunch the next day, there was an empty toilet paper roll on his desk by the phone.

"Now who in the hell would put something like that on my desk?" he asked out loud.

"What did you say, Sam?" Jimmy Frost was passing by.

"Nothing, Jimmy. Just talking to myself. How's your folks?"

"Fine. They're coming home next week. I think it's safe now."

"Good. See ya later."

Suddenly, he knew where the roll had come from. He put it in his pocket and headed for the basement. It had been awhile since he had been in the basement.

"Come in, it's open."

"Mr. Mulvaney… sir… got a minute?" Sam asked.

"For you, Sam, any time. Got my message, huh?"

"Why didn't you just call me?"

"Oh, that wouldn't have been any fun. At least this way, I make you have to think!" The older man smiled.

"You and Jimmy Frost go to the same school?"

"What?"

"Never mind… what have you got for me?"

"Remember when I said you guys are always leaving papers out for me to read late at night?"

"Yeah, I remember."

"This is a copy of a post-it note I found on the mayor's desk last night. Thought you might be interested." He handed Sam a sheet of paper.

The outline of the three-by-three inch note was clear on the white printer paper. Written on it was the word "Avery" and the number, 011-54-11-374-1106 and $200,000.

"Avery Bruin!" Sam exclaimed.

"That was my thought. The number was a little confusing for a minute, then I remembered when my brother was working in Germany, I used to call him once in awhile. Country Code- City Code- Area Code and Number. It's a phone number. Want to guess where? I looked it up."

"Tell me."

"Buenos Aries, Argentina."

"Joe... you are the best!"

"I think I know where Avery Bruin is," Sam said softly. After leaving the janitor, he had gone directly to Captain Boldery's office.

"You do? Where?" His face reflected his shock.

"South America. Buenos Aries, to be exact."

"You sure?"

"Pretty sure. How can we get him back here?"

"I'll see if I can find out." Boldery picked up the phone and dialed. "Yes, Agent Dirkson, please." He put a hand over the mouthpiece. "FBI friend. He should know."

Chapter 50

The United 747 touched down at 6:45 P.M. and taxied to a stop at the gate at the Ministro Pastarini International Airport in Buenos Aries. It had been a pleasant flight; seated in the bubble… the first time Sam had ever had the experience of flying Business Class. *I need one of these seats in my living room*, he thought, caressing the smooth leather as he enjoyed a glass of wine.

"Any flight over six hours, policy says you get to go Business or First class. It's your lucky day," so said Captain Boldery when he dropped Sam's ticket on his desk.

Sam and George Dirkson of the FBI had had seven and a half hours to discuss how they would go about arresting Avery Bruin and bringing him back to the United States. The Argentina National Police had no desire to keep a fugitive in their country, but would not make an arrest until the Americans were there… taking the position of assisting… not initializing. They were met by two officers in military uniforms at the top of the jet way. Introductions were made.

"Is it always this hot?" Sam asked. It had to be in the nineties with a lot of humidity.

"This is our cool season," the older of the two men replied, smiling.

"So, you have our man under surveillance?" Agent Dirkson asked.

"Yes, senor. He has not left his hotel room all day." The younger man, who was introduced as Inspector Gonzalles, answered.

"All day?" Sam was instantly suspicious. He was a very good cop.

"Yes, senor… all day."

"Does the hotel have a restaurant?"

"No… I don't believe it does, senor."

Sam looked at Dirkson. "I smell a rat."

"Yeah. Either he's not there… or somebody else found him first."

"Those are my thoughts exactly."

"I will call my man," Gonzalles responded. There was no answer.

The two Americans barely fit into the back seat of the police car. Sam tried to discover the make of the vehicle, but was unable to find any names or logos. The older of the two *policia* drove. It was like being in a demolition derby. Whoever got to the corner first had the right of way… no matter what. Traffic lights… they were for suggestions only.

The hotel was old and dirty. There was no clerk behind the reception counter. They found the undercover policeman, who was supposed to be watching Avery Bruin, appearing to be asleep in the lobby. His legs propped up on a small table and his face covered with a newspaper. Inspector Gonzales was furious as he yelled at the man to wake up. When he never moved, Gonzales slowly removed the paper to reveal a small hole in the man's forehead. He was very dead. Gonzales said a few Spanish curse words.

"We're too late. He's either dead or gone!" Sam said, as the group raced for the elevator.

"What floor?" Sam asked.

"Nine… 904," came the answer.

No matter how many times they pushed the button, the elevator door would not open. Inspector Gonzales shouted. "Stairs!" and the four policemen took off.

By the time the group reached the ninth floor, Sam was sure he was having a heart attack.

The door to Bruin's room was ajar. With weapons drawn, the local cops pushed the door the rest of the way open, looked back at the two Americans, and begin to holster their guns. Indeed… they were too late. Avery Bruin had a similar hole in his forehead… and for good measure, one in his heart as well. Rangell Alveros would have to find herself another boyfriend. Sam collapsed on the couch, hoping his breath would soon return. He stared at the dead man as the reality of the moment crept into his brain. Bruin was dead. No help from him, that was for sure.

A little while later, the clerk was found in a back room, similarly shot to death.

Chapter 51

"How do they do it, George?" They were two hours into the return flight. Both men had been lost in thought for most of that time, feeling severe disappointment. Finding their fugitive dead had been an unexpected shock. "How do the bad guys seem to always get there first?"

"Probably a drug connection," the FBI agent offered.

"Drugs? These people don't do drugs. At least not the ones I'm trying to nail for this conspiracy thing."

"Well, you said they had a high-priced lawyer from the city. Who do you think the drug guys hire to help them launder their money and take care of their legal problems? High-priced lawyers, that's who. So, if a semi-legitimate business man needs someone out of the way, they call their lawyer and he calls his buddy the drug guy. They have contacts all over the place… especially in South America. Simple procedure. At least that's the theory."

"I need a drink." He stopped a passing flight attendant. "Miss, could I have a vodka on the rocks please?" Sam Gretch was perplexed. Perhaps the vodka would help.

When the two men reached the security exit into the terminal at O'Hare, Sam was rewarded by a very pleasant sight. Beatrice Martin was waiting and had never looked more ravishing. The two embraced warmly and kissed.

"Why don't you two get a room?" agent Dirkson teased.

"I think we can wait another hour. Thanks for picking me up." Sam gave her another kiss. "George, this is Beatrice. Can we drop you someplace?" Sam offered.

"No, I'll just take a cab to the office. I have to file a report on our wasted trip. Boss is going to be pissed that we came back with nothing. Thanks anyway. Nice meeting you, miss." With that he was gone into the crowd.

"So, Bruin was already dead?" Sam had called her from the Buenos Aries Airport.

"Shot right in the middle of the forehead… and, in the heart. He was as dead as they get."

"What about the police down there?"

Sam shook his head. "That would have been a waste of time. A scum bag American killed. No big thing for them. They promised to call if anything comes up on the case. I'm not going to hold my breath on that one!"

"Why don't we stop here in the bar and have a drink? I have some news," Beatrice suggested.

"I thought we were in a hurry to get naked and make a sticky mess out of things."

"We are… but I need to tell you this… and I think you will want to be sitting down."

They found the Windy City Airport Lounge and took a table near the rear. After the drinks were delivered, Sam spoke. "Okay… I'm sitting down. Tell me."

"Linda Ross is dead."

Sam couldn't believe it. "What?"

"She was found this morning, hanging from her brassier tied to the top of her cell door."

"Holy shit! She committed suicide?"

"Well, it did seem like that at first. Somebody sure wanted it to look like suicide. But, Jimmy Frost doesn't think so. He handled the preliminary investigation in your absence. He thinks she was murdered, but he doesn't have much to prove it."

Sam took a long drink. "Jimmy Frost?"

"Yes… he wants you to call him right away."

Sam retrieved his cell and dialed Jimmy's number. He answered on the first ring.

"Yeah, I'm back. Beatrice just told me. What have you got?"

"Well, Sam, she didn't kill herself, that much I know. Her feet were four inches above the turned over chair on the floor. Someone hung her up there, and then turned over the chair to make it looked like she had done it herself. No way to prove it, though."

"Man… she was the last of my witnesses! Fuck! The bastards got to all of them!"

Chapter 52

Six Months Later

Robbie waited patiently in the visitor's room. He had been coming every two weeks, bringing magazines, printer paper and whatever else Noah requested. As always, everything was examined carefully before being handed over to his brother. Having witnessed how careful they were, he hadn't tried the file in the cake thing.

"Hey, bro… how ya doin'?"

"Okay, Robbie. Not bad, I guess. So far I've managed to stay out of trouble. Dodging the perverts and keeping the guards happy is a full-time job. Harley is a good mentor, though. He loves cashews, by the way. Next time, bring him a large can, will you?"

"Sure. No problem. Hey, I got a job!"

"Well, finally! Where?"

"Sweet's Lumber Yard. I'm making deliveries. I really enjoy it."

"That's great. That's nice. I'm happy for you." He was genuinely pleased. "Will you mail this for me? I don't want to spend what little money I have for postage." He handed Robbie a large envelope.

"What's this?"

"A manuscript."

"What's it about?"

"Me."

"What's the title?"

"Noah's Boat Sank."

"Really?"

"No, not really," Noah responded. Robbie was easily duped. "The real title is "My Favorite Truths… Justice, Santa Claus and the Tooth Fairy."

"You're kidding me, aren't you?"

"Yes, dear Robbie… I'm kidding you. It's called *A Matter of Innocence*."

"Am I in it?"

"Sure… you're the main character!"

"People like me …we ain't never the main character."

Noah smiled. "You're right. Maybe next time."

"Okay… I'll hold you to that. I'm going squirrel hunting Sunday."

"Good. Good for you."

"The mortgage company is taking back your house. I took most of your stuff to a storage barn over on Jefferson. I didn't know what to do with Linda's stuff, so I called her niece to come over and get it. I don't know whether she did or not. Your gun safe is at my house."

"Thanks, Robbie. I still can't believe what all's happened in the last year. Me in prison,.. Linda dead. How quickly a person's life can change."

"Yeah. What a bummer."

Chapter 53

The case was getting really cold. There had been absolutely nothing new to look at for six months. As far as the legal system was concerned, John Pritchard's murderer was in prison, where he belonged. Linda Ross's death was still a mystery… but there was no other evidence to support the theory that it was not suicide, even though no one could explain how she was able to hang herself three inches higher that she could have stood…and, Avery Bruin was a fast-fading memory. Most of Sam's fellow policemen didn't even remember the few days he was there. Back with nothing to do, Sam's days were getting longer and longer. Thank God for Beatrice.

Jimmy Frost, on the other hand, was always busy. Armed robberies were up, drug busts were up and a barrage of other crimes surfaced every day.

It was after eleven on a Monday night and he was in the police station filling out last week's paperwork. The call came in from the main switchboard inadvertently to his extension. Anybody who would be calling him at this hour had to be a buddy or a horny girlfriend.

"Yeah," he answered.

"I know I'm not supposed to call you here, but we need to talk. Can you come in tomorrow?"

He did not recognize the voice. "Who are you looking for?"

There was a moment of silence as the caller realized he was not talking to his intended recipient, followed by a loud click. *A wrong number... or was it*. Curious, Jimmy dialed 9 then 7 to reconnect with the calling number. He got a recording.

"You have reached the law office of Orville Merrell. Our office hours are eight to five, Monday through Friday. If this is an emergency, you can call our answering service at..." He hung up and dialed the dispatcher.

"Greg, who was that last call intended for?" Pause "Okay, thanks." *Better leave him a note*, he thought.

Hey...,

You got a call from Orville Merrell. We had a nice talk about similar living styles.

You should call him,

Jimmy

He left the note on the desk in the next office and chuckled as he walked out the door. Similar living styles... that should bring a laugh.

Chapter 54

Sam was going over Noah Ross' file for the hundredth time. Nothing new in there. Nothing new with the conspiracy theory, either.

He put the file in his desk drawer, noticing the cold case file that had mysteriously appeared on his desk his first day as detective. He hadn't looked at it since Pritchard's murder. Now, that seemed like an eternity ago. Out of boredom, he opened it up and began reading.

August 4, 1994. Donald Anderson, thirty-nine years old, partner in Anderson and Anderson Insurance Agency, was found shot to death outside a local motel at eleven thirty on a Tuesday night by a police officer, of all people. A police officer named Frank Boldery. Boldery reported that he received an anonymous call that there was body in the bushes. Turned out it was Mr. Anderson, shot just under the left ear at close range with a large caliber hand gun,

In the ensuing investigation, the police were unable to establish either motive or any suspects in the shooting. The police mainly being Sgt. Frank Boldery. The murder weapon was never found.

Sounds like Dad, Sam thought.

The report was brief and offered no speculations. Sam looked at the black and white photos of the autopsy. The hole under the man's ear was about the size of a dime. The hole in his forehead where the bullet exited was about the size of a half dollar. There were powder burns around the entrance wound.

Poor sucker. Whoever killed him had the gun pressed right against him, Sam thought. *I've nothing else to do... I'll go see his brother.*

The Anderson and Anderson Insurance Agency was still doing business. Sam parked the car, entered the small office, and approached the nondescript woman at the reception desk.

"Hi, can I help you?"

"Yes, is there a Mr. Anderson around?"

"Yes, Eric is here. May I say who is calling?"

"I'm Detective Sam Gretch." He held out his shield.

"Oh! Of course. Just a moment please." She was up and gone in an instant.

Sam smiled. The reaction of the innocent never ceased to amuse him when they saw he was a policeman. Most people, he knew, never had to deal with the police.

She was back with a middle aged man in a golf shirt.

"I'm Eric Anderson. Is there something wrong, sir?"

"No, nothing like that. I'd like to talk to you about Donald. I know he was your partner. Were you two related?"

"Donald! Yes, he was my brother. Perhaps we should go into my office. What did you say your name was?"

"Sam Gretch. I'm a homicide detective." The two moved into a small office and the door was closed.

"Don was murdered nearly ten years ago. Is there something new in all this?"

"Probably not, Mr. Anderson. I'm just reviewing some of our cold cases and had some questions."

"Questions? God, I answered a million questions. Didn't somebody write them down?"

"Yes, of course, sir, although I must admit the report was rather brief. Tell me about your brother."

"He was three years younger than me. He worked hard and played harder... he drank a lot... and he chased a lot of women. I always figured the latter was what got him killed."

"You mean... he played around a bit?"

"A bit? Don was single... good looking... and a charmer. He loved to go after the married ones. I think he figured he was safe... with the married ones."

Sam's interest sparked. "Was he having an affair, you know, when he was killed?"

"I'm sure he was. Rumor had it he was messing around with some cop's wife. The officer in charge of the investigation checked it out. Said as far as he could find out, it was just a rumor."

Sam was confused. There had been no mention of a possible affair with a cop in the report.

"So, why do you think your brother was murdered, Mr. Anderson?"

"Nobody likes my opinion about that."

"Why is that?"

"I think the cops were covering for one of their own. I think the rumor was true. I think the cop whose wife my brother was screwing found out and killed him. That's what I think!"

Sam had an uneasy feeling in his gut. Eric Anderson could be right. Cops covering for other cops. Happens all the time. *Maybe that's why Boldery doesn't want* me *looking into this case. Could he be involved in a cover-up somehow? No! There's no way! Bullshit. Of course there's a way.*

Chapter 55

At nine forty-five the next morning the phone on his desk rang.

"Detective Gretch."

"Detective… my name is … well, never mind. I shouldn't tell you my name. I have some information you want. In exchange for this information, I want to be assured that I will not be involved in any way… that no one will ever know where this information came from."

"What type of information are we talking about? What does it pertain to?"

"A certain group of people… and a football stadium."

Sam nearly fell out of his chair. This man had definitely gotten his full attention.

"I'm listening," he breathed.

"I have documents… copies of correspondence between the principals… the land owners… and the law firm that was negotiating the details."

"I know all those people already. There was nothing illegal in trying to build a new stadium here in this city."

"No, perhaps not. Not at first."

Sam sensed the man had more. "Tell me… what have you really got?"

"I have copies of correspondence… where the principles are discussing how to get around certain board members of the local bank that were opposed to this new stadium… what their options were."

Sam's breathing quickened. "Options… what do you mean by options?"

"There were three options listed in one of the document I have: Option A: Convince the dissenting board members how much good this would do for the community. Option B: Buy the dissenting board members out… then replace them. A figure of five hundred thousand was the proposed buy out amount. Option C: If the above failed, have them eliminated."

Sam could hardly breathe. "Were there names in this document… identifying the people to be eliminated?"

"Yes, sir. Two names… John Pritchard and Arthur Frost."

"Wow. Who initiated these documents?"

"Orville Merrell."

Sam almost wet his pants. "Why are you doing this? Why are you willing to share this with me after all this time?"

"If I tell you that, you will be able to find out who I am. I can't take that chance. If I did, my life would be in danger."

"If you give me the documents you claim to have, won't I be able to figure that out anyway?"

"Perhaps… perhaps not. But, if you do, I want your word you will not disclose my identity to anybody, or I will provide proof the documents are false… and you will have nothing. Who I am is of no importance to you."

"Are the documents false?"

"No, they're authentic. But, I can make them seem to be false… if I need to."

"I see. When do we meet?"

"We don't meet. There is no need to meet. Can you make a case for conspiracy to commit murder with the documents as I have described?"

"I think so. I will need to talk to the State Attorney first… to be sure."

"You shouldn't do that."

"Why not? They have the burden of proving all this at trial."

"I'm aware of the responsibilities here, Detective Gretch. That is not the problem. The problem is… you have no idea how far the tentacles of a certain law firm can reach. If and when this comes to trial, you will have to be very selective…very selective, mind you, regarding who is assigned as the prosecuting attorney."

Sam let that tidbit sink in. *Merrell has a mole in the State Attorney's Office. Of course, he would.* "So… are you going to let me in on who I can trust?"

"The top official in that office, and his number one assistant, along with their wives… were in attendance at Orville Merrell's surprise birthday party last November."

"Holy shit! The top two?"

"Yes, I'm afraid so."

"How about Gordon Sterns?"

"It will be hard to convince him that his boss is… how shall we say… hired help? He would be your best bet, however."

"Can you help me convince him?"

"I don't know. I'll have to think about that. I told you I don't want to be publicly involved."

"Okay, fair enough. I'll give it a try."

"Fine. I will call you again… after you have a chance to discuss it with Sterns. Good day to you, sir."

Sam shoved the cold case file in the drawer. The conspiracy game was back on. It was if he had suddenly become re-charged. For months nothing... then in a matter of minutes, it was all here. All at his fingertips. *Go slow... don't leap into something and fuck this all up. Go slow.*

He drove over to Beatrice's office near the Elmhurst State Bank where this all started. Beatrice was not with a client and would be right out, so assured her secretary. A few minutes later, she appeared.

"Detective Gretch... what a pleasant surprise! Please, come on in. Paige, please hold my calls."

Once the door was safely closed, they embraced and kissed. Both had decided months ago to keep their relationship as formal as possible when in the venues of any part of the legal scene. Although most people knew they were an item, they did not want to taint the system in any way with their personal adventures.

"This is a pleasant surprise, Sammie. I've been thinking about you all day!"

"Yeah, me too... until I got a phone call."

"What?"

"Sit down, baby. Like you told me once... I got news."

Chapter 56

The two lovers spent the next three hours discussing the situation. Beatrice was very familiar with Gordon Sterns… having done battle with him on the Noah Ross case, as well as a few others.

"We'll have to first prove his boss is a rotten bastard traitor."

"How do we do that?" Sam asked.

"What if we were… honest with him. Tell him everything… about everything."

"What if he doesn't believe us?"

"Why would he not believe us?"

"I don't know. I'm not sure I would believe us. The State Attorney… in the pocket of Chicago's most notorious lawyer? That could be hard to believe," Sam said.

"He's a politician, isn't he? What's so hard to believe about that?"

"Not all politicians are bad."

"What did you just say?"

"Yeah… pretty stupid of me, huh? Okay, I'll set up a meeting."

Gordon Sterns graduated from the University of Illinois with honors. Although not from a school noted for turning out the kind of lawyers that demanded the high pay of the large private firms, he was proud of his scholastic accomplishments and was pleased when he was hired into the staff of the Illinois State Attorney's Office. He had proven himself to be a good prosecutor, losing only one out of nine cases in the three years he had been practicing law. After another two more years of experience on this side of the judicial system, he was planning to open his own firm to represent the accused. After five years, he should have a good understanding of how he, the enemy, worked.

He pulled up the collar on his all-weather coat and dashed the two blocks to the Berghoff... the famous Chicago German restaurant he frequented often for lunch. It had been raining all morning... a cold rain that complemented the ten-mile-an-hour wind like a small whip beating him on the cheeks. Safely inside, he shook the drops off his coat and took a seat at the counter.

He was half way through his schnitzel sandwich when Sam Gretch sat down next to him.

"Good afternoon, Counselor."

"Detective Gretch! What are you doing in the city?"

"Came to see you. That sandwich any good?"

"Yes, it's very good. You came to see me?"

"Yes, sir... I did. Nasty weather, isn't it?"

Gordon Sterns smiled. "You came here to discuss the weather. Hah! Why are you being so charming, Detective? I don't remember charm being your normal demeanor."

"No? I always considered myself a charmer."

"A charmer, for sure." He smiled. "If you came to see me, why are we not having this conversation in my office?"

"Because, they serve lousy schnitzel sandwiches in your office... and I wanted to talk to you in private... about a very sensitive subject."

"You have captured my interest. What would this subject be?" He took a bite and chewed slowly.

"Well, like I said, it's very private. I'm sure others from your office come here for lunch from time to time. At least, I would think so."

"Yeah… I'm sure they do."

"Well, are there any of those types around today?"

"You are serious?"

"Serious as I can be."

"Well, I don't see anyone from the office. But, to be sure, I'll make a trip to the restroom. I can see the entire restaurant that way."

"Good idea." Gordon Sterns left his seat and Sam ordered a schnitzel sandwich and a beer from the waitress. Both his order and Sterns arrived back at the same time.

"Okay, what is this all about?" Sterns finished the last of his lunch.

"Well, I'm sure you remember the conspiracy case I was working on during Noah Ross' trial. That's what this is all about. There is a man who claims to have documents that will incriminate Preston Broderick, Helen Pritchard, the mayor of Elmhurst… and Orville Merrell, in a conspiracy to commit murder… the target of which was John Pritchard."

"That's some pretty heavy names. Have you seen these documents?"

"No, but I think this guy is on the up and up. He talks like a lawyer. Like a lawyer who has an axe to grind… like maybe recently being fired by Merrell's firm."

"So, why don't you just get these papers and arrest the conspirators?"

"Well, you see… that's why I needed to talk to you. This guy… the one with the documents… he seems to think your boss is in Orville Merrell's pocket."

"Truesdale? You're full of shit! No way!" Sterns started to leave.

"Wait! What if we can prove it to you… in someway?"

"How would you do that?"

"I don't know yet. I do know that your boss and his assistant were at Orville Merrell's surprise birthday party… with wives. That's a fact."

"That doesn't necessarily mean anything." He didn't sound too convincing.

"Will you help us, or not?"

"You want me to help you take down my boss?"

"No… I have no interest in taking down your boss. I just don't want him to keep me from taking down Orville Merrell. I don't think your boss had any part of this conspiracy."

Sterns settled back in his seat. He spent the next several minutes thinking. Sam spent the next several minutes eating.

"Okay… let's assume for a minute that you're right, and I don't think you are. Perhaps Merrell's law firm was a big contributor during the race for the State Attorney's office. Perhaps, he expects… and perhaps he even gets some special favors from Truesdale. How do I stop my boss from interfering with this case? How do I do that?"

"I don't know, Gordon. That would be up to you. Beatrice Martin and I have discussed this at length. She's the one who suggested that I just tell you the truth. All of it. That's what I have just done."

Sterns was silent for awhile. "When do you plan on doing this thing?"

"After I get the documents. I would like for you to look at them as well. See if we can make this thing stick."

"You're gonna get my ass fired!"

Chapter 57

"Noah, you awake?" Harley asked, trying to keep his voice down.

"Yes. I'm working on my next book."

"I just finished reading the other one. *A Matter of Innocence*... good title. It's good, Noah... better than good... it's great!"

"Thanks, Harley. I hope the publisher thinks so. I was thrilled when they agreed to look at it."

"They would be fools not to publish it. I never considered how easy it would be for somebody to make false evidence to the point where a completely innocent person could be convicted. And, even the policeman who arrested you thinks you are innocent? Incredible! Most evidence is the criminal's own doing... his or her own stupidity. We deserved to get caught."

"You have never told me why you're in here, Harley." There was a pause.

"I know. I'm ashamed of what I did. I don't want to tell you."

"Okay, Harley. That's fine. You don't have to tell me anything."

"Will you two love birds shut the fuck up and go to sleep?" a guy called Forbes yelled from across the way.

"Sure," Noah mumbled, turned off his small light, and found his cot.

At breakfast the next morning, Noah and Harley were joined by a fella named Trellis Moody, a scrawny unshaven man who always looked dirty, even immediately after a shower. He had killed a thirteen-year-old boy for a bicycle, which he promptly sold for drugs. To date, he had served seven years of a life sentence. He sat in silence for the most part of his meal, then laid down his fork and looked into Noah's eyes.

"Why does Harley call you 'Like In the Bible Noah'?"

"It's just a figure of speech. It doesn't mean anything," Noah responded.

"That true, Harley? It don't mean nothin'?"

"Well, Mr. Moody, when Noah came to us… I felt as if we were being sent a sign… an omen. When he said his name was Noah, then I knew that to be true."

"Come on, Harley. That's B.S. and you know it." Noah was amused.

"I been watchin' you. You ain't like the rest of us. I can see that much."

"Mr. Moody, I am not like the rest of you because I didn't commit the crime that they said I did. That's all. I'm not a criminal… and I'm not an omen."

"You're very good with words, you gotta admit that!"

"I'm a writer. A writer is good with words."

"Will you write a letter for me?"

"A letter? What kind of letter."

"A letter to that boy's mom. The one I killed. A letter to her."

"Why don't you write to her?"

He smiled, revealing stained and uneven teeth. "Like you said, 'Like In the Bible Noah'… you are the writer. I don't know what to say."

"You want me to write a letter, but you don't know what to say?"

"Well, I want to say I am sorry. But I don't know how to do that."

"You just did."

Moody frowned and instantly anger flickered in his eyes. "Are you telling me you won't write the letter?"

"Of course he'll write the letter, Mr. Moody," Harley interrupted. "Of course he will."

"Okay, Mr. Moody, let's talk during exercise time. You try to tell me how you feel, and I'll try to write your letter." Noah decided to keep the peace.

That afternoon, the two of them went to a secluded bench away from the other prisoners and they talked… for an hour…they talked. Later that night, Noah wrote the letter. At breakfast the next morning, he handed it to Trellis Moody.

"I hope this is what you had in mind," Noah said.

"Will you read it to me, Harley?" Moody offered the folded letter to Harley.

"Sure, Moody. Glad to."

Harley began to read…slowly, as if he was reading a poem of great renown. Soon, there was a small group of listeners gathered around the three men.

> *Dear Mrs. Wilkins,*
>
> *My name is Trellis Moody. I know that you know who I am, but I need to tell you… I am the monster who took the life of your son, Frankie. I used to blame it on the drugs, but to be honest, there is absolutely no excuse for what I did. None. I will most assuredly rest eternally in hell.*
>
> *I am writing to you because I want you to forgive me. Not for me… because I will*

never forgive myself... but for you. I know what the burden of hate can do to a person. I know that right now, you hate me. You will never be able to get on with your life... to be happy, as you deserve to be, as long as you are filled with hate.

I will spend the rest of my life in prison. Rightfully so. But you must not spend the rest of your life in your own personal prison of hate. That's not right. God will punish me for what I did. There's no need for you to do the same.

I expect you will cry when you read this. That's okay. Cry for Frankie. Cry for your loss. I will do the same.

Trellis Moody

Noah had been watching Trellis carefully as Harley read. At first, he showed no emotion, listening with a stone face. Then a tear began to form and eventually ran over his bottom eyelid and continued down his cheek. When Harley said 'cry for Frankie' he lost it, sobbing like a heartbroken child, his face buried in his hands. There was no other sound. The small crowd around the table was silent... reflecting...in a trance.

Noah was the first to move as he stood and, slowly, walked back toward his cell. *Well... I guess it was all right. I just made a cold blooded murderer cry.*

During the next three months, he received forty three requests to write letters. Some to victims... some to judges... and some to relatives. He rejected some, some he honored. He was even more amused that his nickname had been shortened to Bible Noah.

"I don't deserve the nickname, Harley," he said one day. "I'm only a CEW Christian."

"And, my dear friend, what is a CEW Christian?"

You know… I go to church on Christmas, Easter and weddings."

Chapter 58

Sam and Beatrice had a relaxed dinner at Garland's, quietly discussing his meeting with Gordon Sterns.

"So, you think he may have believed you about his boss?"

"I planted the seed. We'll have to wait and see if it grows. I told him I didn't think his boss was part of the conspiracy thing… I just don't want him to interfere with those who are. I think he bought that much. Hey, Jake, bring us another beer."

"Coming right up, Sam."

"What are you going to do next?"

"Wait. Wait until this guy calls me again. Then, go from there."

"I want you to take a little trip with me… for the weekend."

"To where?"

"Galena. I have an aunt who owns a bed and breakfast there. They go to Florida in the winter and I have a key. We'll have the place all to ourselves."

"I'll need to buy some condoms." He liked the idea. A few days off the job sounded great.

"Get a dozen, Sammie boy. I got big plans for that thingy you keep in your pants."

"My, my, counselor… how you talk!"

They left at six the next morning, driving leisurely, stopping for breakfast near Rockford. Later, they stopped at an antique shop and browsed for another hour. Beatrice bought Sam an antique pipe rack.

"I don't smoke a pipe."

"I know… but this will look nice on your coffee table. You need a little class in that place, Sammie."

"Why don't you move in with me… then the place would have a little class."

"Yeah, right."

"I'm serious."

She was silent, a little bit frightened, not sure of what to say. "Oooh…I'll think about that. I will… definitely think about that."

They arrived in Galena around noon, stopped at a small grocery store and bought things for dinner and snacks and a couple bottles of wine. The house was nice and cozy, once the furnace kicked on and warmed the rooms. They picked an upstairs bedroom with a king-size four poster and a small brick fireplace. Sam lit the gas log and Beatrice opened a bottle of Chardonnay, and then threw a thick comforter on the floor in front of the fire. Sam slipped his shoes off and sat on the floor. Beatrice began unbuttoning her blouse.

"You got way too many clothes on, Sammie. It's time to get naked." She finished removing her blouse and her bra, then cupped her full breasts and shook them at him. "Want some of my sugar?"

This bit of action caused an immediate erection, and he was quick to join her as she removed the rest of her clothes. "Where did I pack those rubbers?" Sam mumbled, struggling to get his jeans off.

"You won't need them for a while. Lay down, Sammie. This first one is all my treat."

They made love all afternoon… in every way either of them could think of. She was insatiable and he was… inspired. As they shared a glass of wine in between one of their sessions, Sam noticed something… a revelation. Beatrice lay on one elbow, her breathing still elevated, her breasts swaying to and fro.

"Bebe… you are ravishing. Have you lost some weight?"

"You can tell?" she asked, pleased.

"Well, you've always been so gorgeous… perfect in every way…but today, I noticed something different. I wouldn't have thought it possible, but you do look even more beautiful than ever before!"

"You sweet, sweet Sammie." She smiled. "You deserve something special. What will it be this time?"

Around six, he began to get hungry. "You want me to fix us some dinner?" he asked.

"Why don't we go out? I know this really neat Italian place… red checkerboard tablecloths and candles in a bottle. It's really romantic… and it's close enough we can walk."

"I'm not sure I can walk. My knees are a bit shaky!"

But walk he did and they had a very nice dinner. One he would remember for a long time.

They ordered a dessert to share, and while they were waiting, Sam asked, "Bebe… tell me something about lawyers."

"Oh, oh. Am I in trouble?"

"No, you are not in trouble." Sam smiled. "When we were coming back from Buenos Airies, I asked the FBI agent how the bad guys knew where Bruin was… so they could kill him before we got there. He said it was probably through their lawyers, who most likely had contacts in the drug trade. That kinda shocked me at first, but it makes sense. He said the large drug dealers could afford the best lawyers and favors are most likely exchanged. What do you think about that?"

Their dessert arrived; a chocolate mound of calories with white goo on top.

"Oh, that looks good!" she remarked, taking a bite. "Unfortunately, he's probably right. The drug cartels and the Mafia types have a lot of money, and they often need legal representation. So, they go to the best... because they can afford them. I know it's an ethics thing... but the big money always wins... and our legal system insures the right for all factions to have access to legal counsel."

"Can't the attorneys refuse to represent a client?"

"Sure, unless they're court-appointed. But when the opportunity to make millions of dollars comes knocking, if the first guy doesn't take it, the next one will." She took another bite. "Dad had an opportunity once, back in the fifties. Mafia group. He turned them down. In the next six months, he lost half of his clients... the best half. He thinks they got phone calls... told to go elsewhere. See... some of us do have scruples! But scruples don't come without a price."

"I've never met your father."

"He's in a nursing home in Lake Geneva. Alzheimer's. Doesn't even know me anymore."

"I'm sorry." Sam was never more sincere,

"Yeah... me too."

When they returned to the house, Sam felt refreshed... and re-armed. He poured them each a glass of wine and was ready to start all over again when his cell phone went off.

"Sam Gretch," he answered. As he listened, his face went white.

"What! Say that again."

"Jesus Christ!" He disconnected. "We got to go, Bebe. Jimmy Frost has been shot!"

Chapter 59

It had taken them four and a half hours to make the trip to Galena. It took them two hours and twenty minutes to make the trip back. Jimmy Frost was still in surgery, so they had been told at the hospital reception desk. Captain Boldery met them when the elevator door opened.

"How's he doing, Frank?" Sam could barely get the words out.

"Not good, Sam. Took one in the neck and one in the midsection. Big caliber… probably a forty four. He's been in surgery for three hours now. They almost lost him in the ER."

"What the hell happened?"

"Well, near as we can determine so far, he had stopped in at the 7-Eleven on Gray Street to get some beer on his way home. Apparently, there was a robbery in progress. According to the clerk, Jimmy pulled his gun on a guy taking money out of the cash register. He yelled at the guy to get down on the floor. The clerk tried to warn him, but before he caught on, a second guy came out of a back room and shot Jimmy in the neck from behind. He went down, and the guy behind the counter shot him in the stomach. Then they ran out."

"Damn! So they ambushed him."

"Yeah. Bummer." The three were interrupted by a doctor dressed in surgery scrubs.

"Captain Boldery?"

"Yes… I'm Boldery."

"I'm Dr. Hammond. Mr. Frost is out of surgery in recovery."

"How is he?" Sam demanded.

"Not good, I'm afraid. He lost a lot of blood at the scene. The wound to the neck has severely damaged his spinal column. If he lives… and I stress, if… he will most likely be paralyzed. We won't know that for several hours."

"Son of a bitch!" Sam collapsed on the waiting room sofa. Beatrice sat at his side and put her arm around him.

"Did Officer Frost say anything? About the shooting?" Boldery asked.

"Yes." The doctor responded. "A couple of times he said… excuse me Ma'am… 'Fuckin' Tacos!' "

"Okay… well, we got someplace to start. Mexican gang, maybe? Thank you, doctor. Please call me if there is any change." He shook hands with the doctor and turned. "You ready to go to work, Sam?"

Chapter 60

Sam dropped Beatrice off at her place, promised he would indeed be careful, and headed for the 7-Eleven. The young Pakistani clerk was still quite upset. Nothing like this had ever happened to him before.

"How is the policeman who was shot?" he asked.

"He's alive... that's about all," Sam answered. "You want to tell me about it?"

"I already tell everything to the first officers."

"Yeah, I know. Officer Frost...the guy that was shot... he is a very good friend of mine. Now, you tell *me* everything."

"He comes in every night, your friend. Almost every night, anyway. He gets a six pack of Bud Lite and sometimes other things. But always, the Bud Lite. The Spanish guys... they come in and wait... looking at the magazines, drinking cokes... talking in Spanish. One goes into the restroom. I am getting nervous. I think maybe they are going to rob me. But they wait. They are here for over half hour."

"Are you saying they were waiting for Officer Frost to come in?"

"Perhaps it is possible. I think so."

"Jesus Christ!" Sam was pissed. This was not an interrupted robbery. This was a planned assassination! "Okay, go on."

"The short one...the one with the scar on his head, he show me a gun and say to be quiet to anybody. He stands here by the counter. The other one still waits in the restroom. When your friend comes in, he goes to the beer cooler in the back, and the man here comes over the counter and tell me to open cash register. I do as told. Your friend, the policeman, see what is going on, holds up a badge and points his gun at the man. He shouts for him to get on the floor. I see the other man come from the restroom with a gun. I try to warn the policeman… but he does not look. The man from the restroom shoots your friend and he falls to the floor. Then the man behind counter… he shoots him also. Then they run from the store."

"Did they take any money?"

"No… they did not take money."

"Okay." It was a definite ambush. "Thank you, son. You did good. Tell me about the scar."

"The scar?"

"Yes… you said the man behind the counter had a scar on his head. What did it look like?"

"Oh… like the letter J, over his left ear."

Sam left the store and went to the police station, where he called the hospital and was told there was no change.

Jimmy Frost's desk was unlocked. Sam started a drawer-by-drawer search… looking for any file on Hispanic gangs or drug deals. The desk was a mess… typical Jimmy. There were no tabs on any of the fifty or so file folders, and they were all the same color. Jimmy used to joke that he filed everything under 'M' for miscellaneous. Sam was starting to believe that was actually true. It took an hour to go through everything in the desk. As far as he could tell, there was nothing related to his shooting in any of the files. Nothing.

Sam left the station and drove to the hospital. Every policeman carried a note book. Perhaps he could find something there. He finally convinced a reluctant nurse to give him Jimmy's personal effects; a wallet containing thirty-four dollars, a ring of keys, a small pocket knife and a small notebook. There were phone numbers, around twenty, including his and Beatrice's, as well as the number for Garland's bar. There were notes of interviews with suspected drug dealers, the code word to get into the local whorehouse, and various bits of other information important to a person in Jimmy's job… but, there were no entries that had anything to do with a Mexican or Cuban gang. Another dead end.

Chapter 61

"Noah, you awake?" he whispered.

Noah looked at his watch. 2:07 a.m. "What is it, Harley?"

"I've decided to tell you."

"Tell me what?"

"Why I'm here."

"Oh. Okay."

"You can't write about it."

"Okay, Harley. I won't write about it."

"I killed her, Noah. I loved her, but I killed her. I almost got away with it, too."

Noah wasn't sure what to say. "Why did you kill her, Harley?"

"She just wouldn't shut up. Always harping at me… get a job, quit drinkin', do this do that. One day, I had had enough. I went to the garage and got the hatchet. She was washing dishes in the sink. I came up behind her and hit as hard as I could on top of the head. Damned near split her head in two!"

Noah was silent, not used to this mild-mannered man talking like this.

"I cut her up, Noah. Made her into little bitty pieces. Took all the meat off the bones and ground it up in the garbage disposal. Then I took the bones down to the basement and burnt them in the furnace until they were gone. It took four days to burn her head. That was the hardest. The kitchen was a mess. I mopped and washed… then soaked everything down in bleach. God, did that smell! I told everybody she left. Went to Maine to be with her sister.

They believed me." He stopped long enough to blow his nose. "It was so peaceful. Just me in the house. Then her sister came. She didn't call or nothin'... just showed up with her suitcase... askin' questions. I remember getting real nervous. I figured I'd have to do her too. I was afraid, Noah...really afraid. I went to my bedroom and locked myself in. She called the police. But, I was cool, Noah. I had them convinced she had just left... told me she was going to her sister's and left. Since she obviously didn't go to her sister's, I didn't have any idea where she went. They were all believing me... except for the sister. She moved into the spare bedroom and decided to stay for awhile. I hated her... but what could I do?" Harley went on... at times seeming to talk more to himself than to Noah.

"Then, the damned garbage disposal stopped. Burnt the motor up. I called a plumber guy to replace it, and right in front of her sister... he finds this ring... her ring...stuck in the gunk in the drain. She called the cops again, and this time, they tested the goop the ring was in. Well, it was all down-hill from there. They found bone fragments in the furnace and blood on the hatchet. I had almost made it. Damned sister!"

"That's terrible, Harley. Terrible. Although, you're certainly not the first to get so angry at their wife that they killed her, I guess I don't understand that kind of anger. I was so angry at my wife once... but I could never have harmed her."

"It wasn't my wife, Noah." He hesitated for effect. "It was my mother."

"What?" He hadn't been prepared for that.

"Yes... unfortunately. But I learned a valuable lesson from all that, Noah."

He was in shock… almost unable to believe what he had just heard. "And, what lesson was that, Harley?" he asked.

"Well, I'll never use *that* damned plumber again!"

There was silence for a minute… then a snicker from down the way… then a few giggles… then the cell block erupted with laughter. Finally, Noah realized he had just been had… by his new, best friend.

"Harley… you are an absolute ass!"

"Gotcha, huh, Noah!"

Chapter 62

Sam Gretch was frustrated. For three days he had done nothing but try to find out information on Jimmy's shooters. The Gang Squad, as they called the Chicago police unit dealing with these kinds of problems, had nothing on a man with a scar on his head.

Jimmy was still in a coma. A machine was breathing for him and he had not moved a muscle since being admitted. Sam had spent most of every night sitting at his side. Waiting. Hoping. Praying. Some times he was joined by Jimmy's friends, Rudy and George, from the fire station. They wouldn't stay as long as he did, but every time they came, the conversation turned to the time they outran the Harbor Police in Jimmy's boat.

On the fourth night, at 3:10 a.m., Jimmy Frost died. The machine kept on wheezing and hissing, but Jimmy was gone. The air coming out of his nose started to make a different kind of sound. Sam called the nurse and she confirmed his fears. There was no pulse. The heart had stopped. She flipped a switch and the wheezing stopped as well.

Sam had been in Garland's for three hours. He was sitting in their favorite booth… as far back in the room as possible, drunk out of his senses. Jake called Beatrice.

"Beatrice… you'd better come and get him. He won't let me call a taxi and he insists I keep the drinks coming."

"Be right there, Jake."

Ten minutes later, she slid in the seat opposite him. "Come on, big guy, time to go home."

"Hi, Bebe! When did you get here?"

"Just a few minutes ago. You ready to go home?"

"Jimmy died. Just quit livin'. He was still breathing…but he was dead. Ain't that something?" He took another drink.

"I know, honey. I know."

"If they got fuckin' machines that can breathe for ya, why don't they have fuckin' machines to keep your heart goin'?"

"I don't know honey. Let's go home and talk about this in the morning."

"What time is it?"

"Almost ten o'clock."

"Jimmy died, Bebe."

"I know, Sam. I'm very sorry."

"I'm going to throw up." And throw up he did.

Chapter 63

The funeral was in Naperville, a few miles west of the city. Even though Jimmy's parents were very wealthy, it was a simple service, one Jimmy would have wanted. There were around seventy-five policemen and firefighters in attendance, and a hundred or so friends and relatives. Jimmy had never married. Just as well. It's not an easy experience to be a police widow.

After the service, Sam and Beatrice were invited to the family home. There was the usual array of food and drinks and sad conversations. Arthur Frost was a gracious host, in spite of the circumstances. He was a tall man, nearly six foot six, and deeply tanned. His tailored cashmere suit fit perfectly and he was as polished as his five hundred dollar shoes. He fixed two vodka rocks and approached Sam, offering one to the policeman.

"Detective, could I talk to you in private?"

"Of course, Mr. Frost."

"Come with me, please." The older gentleman led the way into a room which was obviously the library and shut the door. In spite of the circumstances, Sam could not help thinking how nice it must be to have a house with a library.

"Do you have any idea who is responsible for my son's murder?"

"All we have is the description from the store clerk… no names, and no motive. I'm working on it… but I'm afraid I don't have much to go on yet."

"Jimmy and I talked about the bank thing, you know. The conspiracy, if you will. Perhaps, since it would have been too obvious to have me... killed, they have chosen to kill Jimmy... to bring me in line before the next vote."

Sam had not considered that. "It's possible," he said, thoughtfully. "My original feeling was that this was revenge for something Jimmy had done to a gang... or drug related. I might be looking in the wrong direction."

"Well, if that is the reason for Jimmy's murder, it worked. I will no longer oppose the rest of the board. In fact, I will most likely resign my position soon."

"Mr. Frost, I can certainly understand where you're coming from...but, please...don't resign just yet. It's okay to vote with them, that will remove you from danger, but it would be nice to have a contact inside the board meetings to let me know what is going on."

"Very well, I will do as you ask. If I am correct... I want these people to pay. I want them to pay dearly. Will you see to that, Detective Gretch?"

"I'll do my best, sir."

"Good. If you need resources that are not available to you... perhaps that require money, you let me know."

"Yes, sir. That won't be necessary."

"I was against him becoming a policeman, you know."

"Sir?"

"My Jimmy. I wanted him to be... well, something else. Certainly not a cop. I don't mean that disrespectfully."

"I understand, sir."

"Good. I don't mean to offend you, Detective. Lord knows we need good policemen. It's just...

well, I've always been afraid something like this would happen."

"I'll do the best I can to get his killers, Mr. Frost. Jimmy was my best friend."

"Very well. I must go and visit with the others now. Please excuse me."

Sam watched him walk away with a certain degree of pity. *Even the very wealthy have pain*, he thought. He finished his vodka in one swallow and went to find another. He too was feeling pain for the loss of his friend.

Chapter 64

Most of the day on Monday, Sam spent going over the file on Spanish speaking gangs the Chicago Police had sent over. There was absolutely nothing he could find that would connect any of the gangs with Jimmy… or the bank… or any members of the bank's board of directors.

He slipped out for a burger at Garland's around noon, and when he returned there was another empty toilet paper roll on his desk. He smiled, threw it in the trash and headed for the basement.

"Joe? You there?" He knocked on the door.

"Enter, esteemed one…enter!" came the muffled reply.

"What's up?"

"Sorry about Jimmy. I know you two were close."

"Yeah, thanks. I'm going to miss him."

"Any progress on his case?"

"No. Nothing but dead ends."

"I don't know if it means anything or not. I'm not a policeman. But, apparently, Boldery got a call the other night, and Jimmy answered it. I found this on Boldery's desk. I made this copy." He handed the note to Sam. He read it carefully. Why would Frank Boldery be getting a call from Orville Merrell?

Later that evening, he was ready to call it a day when his phone interrupted.

"Detective Gretch."

"Yes... it's me. Did you get a chance to talk with Gordon Sterns?"

"I did." Sam had to switch his mind into another mode. "He is willing to help as long as we are not going after his boss."

"That's no problem. Other than accepting a large campaign donation, I don't think the State's Attorney is involved with the Merrell firm. I just don't want him to interfere."

"He wants to see the documents before we proceed. I told him he could."

"I'll send you a copy to your home address. I should explain...these are hard copies of e-mails. When you are ready to make arrests, you will have to confiscate the individual computers. The originals will still be on their hard drives, even if they have deleted them."

"How were you able to acquire these e-mails?"

There was a pause. "Okay, if you must know, I was the firm's communications expert. Fixed all their computer problems and set up their different software files. I even know all their passwords."

"You said... was?"

"Yes. Was. I was fired... for having an affair with the wife of one of the partner's. It was just a physical thing with me. She came on to me, and I responded. He caught us. I was fired. That's it."

"Okay... now that I know how to find out who you are, why don't you give me a number where I can reach you? I'll call you after I've read the e-mails."

"Why not. I've nothing to lose, now. My name is Lawrence Coverett. My number 977-7866."

Sam stopped in at Garland's and had a beer while apologizing for the mess he had made a few nights before. The beer didn't taste good and everything in there reminded him of the good times he had had with Jimmy.

"You want something to eat, Sam?" Jake asked.

"Naw… not hungry. I think I'll just go home." He threw a five on the bar and left.

It was snowing hard… huge flakes, the kind that blind you in the headlights. He was sliding all over the road on the way home and nearly took out a mailbox… like the one where Noah's gun was found. Poor Noah… just another source of depression.

When he turned the key to his apartment, the door locked instead of unlocking. It had already been unlocked. He could think of no reason it should be and his internal alarm went off. He drew his gun and turned the key again, then entered the dark entryway.

"Anyone here?" he asked loudly.

"Just me, Sammie. Don't trip over my suitcases."

"Bebe? Suitcases?"

"You did ask me to move in, didn't you?"

She was sitting in his recliner, covered with a throw.

"Yeah, I did, didn't I?" He shut the door and put his gun away. "I'm afraid I'm not in a very good mood, Bebe."

"Well, I bet I can change that!" She stood and the throw ended up in the floor, revealing her nakedness.

And change it she did.

Chapter 65

The next morning it took him thirty minutes to shovel a path to the street. It had snowed almost a foot of the white, poofy stuff overnight. Everything looked so new… pure and white. It did make him feel better… a feeling that was short-lived. When he swept the snow off his windshield, he found a wet sheet of paper with smeared writing, stuck under the wiper blade.

Policeman Gretch,
We have fixed your friend. We will fix you soon.
Bet on it.

Being careful not to tear the wet paper from his shaking hands, he laid the note on the front seat. "You fixed my friend, huh? Well, maybe, I won't be so easy to fix, senor," he mumbled to himself.

When he arrived at the police station, the first thing he did was to get his extra gun with the ankle holster and put it on. Sam Gretch was now on his highest alert mode.

He showed the note to Captain Boldery.

"So, this was not a random thing. They wanted Jimmy. And now, they want you. Were you two working on anything together?"

"No… not really. The only connection, other than us being good friends, was that Jimmy's dad is on the board of directors at the bank. He wasn't helping me with anything on that."

"Perhaps, they thought he was."

"Could be," Sam replied thoughtfully.

"You want me to put somebody with you… a temporary partner?"

"No. I don't want anybody else killed on my behalf. I'll do this thing alone."

"Okay. Let me know if you change your mind."

Sam decided to play his trump card. "By the way, did you know that Don Anderson was having an affair with a married women when he was killed?"

"Who?"

"Donald Anderson. You know… my cold case?"

"Why are you fucking around on that? I told you I covered everything." It was clear the man was pissed. He was nearly yelling. Sam had definitely hit a sore spot. He decided to let it drop for now. Other fish to fry at the moment.

"Okay… no big deal."

Chapter 66

The word got around the mess hall quickly. Noah had been finally baptized with the "Mother Down the Drain" story.

"Hey, Bible Noah… know any good plumbers?"

"My sink is stopped up, too… can you help?"

"They're having meatloaf for lunch tomorrow!"

Noah just smiled, not responding to the barrage of remarks.

"Sorry, Noah. They've been wanting me to do that for months now." Harley said as they stood in line for breakfast.

"Okay, friend… have your fun. My turn will come."

"Have you heard anything from the publisher?"

"No, not a thing. They probably didn't like it. I had over thirty rejections on my first book. It never was published."

"Then they are fools. I thought it was excellent."

The two men took their seats at their usual table. Just another typical morning in prison. Nothing could have prepared Noah for what happened next.

The General was walking between the tables headed in their direction, when suddenly; there were three inmates blocking his way. A fellow called Freaky Frankie, along with Crude Lude and a lifer called Habash made a lunge all at the same time. Noah could see a shiny object in his chest as the General dropped his tray of food, and his body followed the loud clatter of dishes to the cement floor. He moved no more.

Noah started to go to him.

"Stop!" Harley whispered, grabbing him by the arm. "Stay out of it!"

"But I saw…"

"You saw nothing! Understand? You saw nothing!"

Noah's heart was racing. He had just witnessed a man stabbed not ten feet away. The three inmates had disappeared. Somebody yelled, and a siren went off. Noah could hear the cell doors in the distance slam shut and guards appeared from every direction, slamming shut the doors to the cafeteria as well, not letting anybody leave or enter.

"Nobody move," one of the guards ordered. "Stay exactly where you are!" The room became deathly silent.

A few minutes later, the warden entered with his assistant and the prison doctor. Noah had seen him before… the warden. A small man with a pock faced complexion, but a man who's aura commanded respect.

The doctor bent and tried to find a pulse. "He's dead, sir," he reported to his boss.

The warden shook his head in understanding, then carefully observed all the nearby prisoners.

"You, you, you and you… stand up. Take these men to a holding cell," he ordered and guards quickly left with the men. The warden turned in Noah's direction. He pointed again. "You, you, you, you and you. Go!" Noah rose and was grabbed by the arm and escorted out of the room.

In the large holding cell, no one said a word. Not one word. One by one, they were taken out of the cell and disappeared down the hall. None of them came back. It was over an hour before Noah was summoned by two guards.

"Let's go, Ross." He was handcuffed and led down the hall, up a set of stairs and into what was obviously the warden's office. A large deer head was on the wall next to a credenza filled with photos and other memories of police buddies, hunting trips and sporting events, making it evident that this was a man's man. A picture of a very attractive middle aged woman was on the large mahogany desk.

"Sit here." The guard directed him to a lone chair in front of the desk. The assistant warden took a seat on the right side of the desk, and the two guards left the room.

Eugene Stroman had been the warden of the Menard facility for eight years now. This was the ninth time a prisoner had been killed during his tenure. He was thoroughly pissed. He opened the file on his desk.

"Noah Ross. Convicted of murder in the first degree. Hmm. No hickies on your record here. Good, clean upstanding citizen, huh Mr. Ross?" There was a bitterness not to be missed in his voice.

"I try to be, sir," Noah answered truthfully.

"I'm told you write letters for people that can't. Is that true?"

"Yes, sir. I've written a few letters."

"Why do you do that, Mr. Ross?"

"I'm a writer, sir. It's easy for me to express… ideas… in words. Just trying to help out, sir."

The warden nodded. Like I said, good, upstanding citizen, aren't you." He paused. "I'm mad, Mr. Ross. Goddamned mad! When I'm mad, people get hurt. You understand me, Mr. Ross?"

"Yes, sir."

"Okay… that's good. Now. Let's pretend that you are writing a letter to Bernard's wife. Or maybe, you know him as the General. How are you going to tell her that he died, Mr. Ross?"

"I… I don't know, sir." Noah said weakly.

The warden slammed his open hand hard on the desk, causing every one in the room to jump. "That's not what I wanted to hear, Mr. Ross. Now," he pointed a shaking finger at Noah, "you tell me what the fuck you saw. Every detail, you understand?"

"Yes, sir… I understand. But, I'm afraid I didn't see who did it. When I turned to look, the General was already on his way down. I did see that he was bleeding."

"Who was near him, Mr. Ross?"

"No one, sir," he lied… hoping he was convincing. "There was no one near him."

"Oh… then you think he stabbed himself?"

"Well, sir, no… I don't think that. I just do not know who did it."

"I don't believe you. Just like the jury didn't believe you. You know… the jury that sent you here?" He directed his attention to his assistant. "Mr. Stark, should we put Mr. Ross in an isolation cell for a few days, to jog his memory? And, suspend his computer privileges till further notice?"

"We could, unless Mr. Ross wants to cooperate."

"Gentlemen, listen to me. If I knew anything that would help with your investigation, I would share that with you. I didn't see who did it. Putting me in the tank will not make me remember something I did not see."

That statement brought a moment of silence to the room, as the warden considered what he had said.

"Very well, Mr. Ross. If I find out different, you will be in for the roughest time of your life, understand? Bring his computer here to me. I want to see what he has been writing about. Get him out of here."

Chapter 67

It had been four days since Sam had talked to Lawrence Coverett about the e-mails. He checked the mail several times each day, but there was nothing there. At four o'clock, he called the number he had been given. There was no answer. An hour later, he called again. No answer.

He met Bebe at Garland's around six and they were having their first beer.

"That guy, Coverett, never sent the e-mails. I'm getting worried," Sam announced.

"Call him," Bebe offered.

"I did. He doesn't answer."

"Better go find him."

"Just what I was thinking. I got his address. He lives in Oak Park. Wanna come with me?"

"Sure. You can buy me dinner in the city!"

It took them forty minutes to make the trip and it was getting dark when they found the apartment building. It was in a nice neighborhood made up of similar, two-story brownstones. The mailbox reported he lived in apartment B on the second floor. The mailbox also showed he hadn't been picking up his mail. It was stuffed full. That was not a good thing. They walked up the stairs and Sam knocked on the door then stepped back.

"Shit! Smell that?" he asked Bebe.

"Yes. Is it what I think it is?" She held a gloved hand over her nose.

He took out his cell phone and called 911. Even though he was a policeman, he had no jurisdiction in Oak Park. From the smell, he now thought he knew why this man had not been picking up his mail.

The body was on the kitchen floor. The rather large black man lay face up in a pool of dried blood. He had a large hole in his chest that appeared to have been made by a knife. A glass of soured milk on the table was not helping with the odor. There was evidence of a struggle; chairs overturned, broken dishes on the floor and blood in several different places.

"Looks like he put up a fight," the Oak Park policeman remarked. "I'd better call homicide. You two… don't go anywhere, and don't touch anything. They will want to talk to you as to why you're here."

"Sure, we aren't going anywhere. Let's sit in the other room, Bebe," Sam suggested. Trying not to bring suspicion, he carefully looked around for any sign of the e-mail documents. There were none in sight… and there was no computer in the apartment either. Strange for a computer expert not to have one at his home.

Seated on the couch, Bebe whispered, "What are you going to do now?"

"That's not our man," he whispered.

"Really?"

He nodded. "I'm pretty sure our man is white."

"So, where is he?"

"I don't know." Sam shook his head. "I just don't know."

Twenty minutes later they were joined by a Chicago homicide detective.

"So, a fellow homicide dick, I'm told. I'm Bret Holloway." The young man returned Sam's I.D.

"Tell me, Detective, what was your relationship with the deceased?"

Sam wasn't especially fond of being called a *dick*... of any kind.

"None, really. I think I was to meet someone else here tonight. A Mr. Lawrence Coverett. He was supposed to have some documents for me... to help in a case I've been working on. A fellow policeman... a friend... was killed a few weeks ago. This guy said he had something for me. He was supposed to send it in the mail. When I didn't get it, I came looking for him. When I got the smell, I called 911. That's it."

"What kind of documents?"

"I don't know. He didn't say," Sam lied.

"Really?" It was obvious that the officer wasn't sure whether or not to believe him. He directed his attention to Bebe. "And you, miss?"

"I was promised a dinner at a nice restaurant in the city. I came along for the ride." Bebe gave him her best "I'm innocent" smile.

"But this guy is not the man you were supposed to meet?"

"Well, I never met the guy... just talked to him on the phone, but I'm pretty sure my man is a Caucasian. So, no, I don't think this is Coverett."

"You guys get an I.D.?" the detective asked one of the uniforms.

"His driver's license says he is Devon Brooks. Got quite a rap sheet, according to central," one of the cops answered.

The detective looked back at Sam. "Well, looks like you're right. Maybe the wrong guy got killed in this meeting." He paused. "Okay. I guess you two can go. I know where to find you if I need to."

"Thank you, Detective Holloway. I appreciate the professional courtesy," Sam said, and meant it.

"No problem. Have a nice dinner."

"By the way… I'm not a fellow *dick*. I'm a policeman."

The young man stood in silence as they walked out of the room. He had been duly corrected.

Chapter 68

At 9:30, they arrived in front of their apartment and started to pull into the drive, but found the way blocked by a three-foot high levee of frozen snow.

"Damned snow plow!" Sam muttered. "Stay in the car, I'll shovel us a way in." He parked the car in the street and made his way to the front porch and the snow shovel. As he started to return to the task, he became aware of a car speeding down the block. Suddenly, an automatic rifle appeared from the passenger side window and began firing."

"Bebe! Get down!" Sam shouted, drawing his own weapon, seeking cover behind the frozen snow bank. The car sped past, the assault rifle continuing to blast away, the bullets sending snow and ice stinging into Sam's face. As soon as it was a few feet down the street, Sam rose on one knee and emptied his forty four at the fleeing car. Windows shattered and the rifle fell to the street, then the car swerved and went out of control, hitting a utility pole, sliding broadside into the passenger door. Sam quickly replaced the empty clip and headed toward the wreck, but slipped on the ice and went down hard, splitting open his left knee on the hard surface. Just as he was able to regain his feet, he saw the driver run down the block and disappear around the corner. Slowly, he limped toward the disabled car, gun ready. There was no movement inside. He could see the man in the passenger seat, slumped over, his head on the dash at a grotesque angle.

"Don't you move, you son of a bitch!" he ordered, panting from exertion and pain.

No worry. The man was not going to move, ever. There were two holes in his neck. One bullet had severed his spine. From the dome light, Sam could see clearly… the man's shaved head and the scar over his right ear… in the shape of a J.

"Well, there's one of 'em for you, Jimmy," he muttered, and at the same time he noticed the blood on the steering wheel. "I hit the other one, too, buddy. But, he's still breathing… for awhile."

"Sam! Are you okay?" Beatrice yelled, from the safety of their car.

He waved an arm to let her know he was not shot. The pain in his knee was bad and he could see blood all over his pants leg. "Call 911, Bebe!" he yelled back. "Tell them we got a DOA and an officer with a broken knee."

Four minutes later, it was like a circus had arrived outside his apartment. Two ambulances, three black and whites, and two plain cars… all with roof lights flashing and radios blaring. One of the unmarked police cars belonged to Captain Boldery.

Sam was sitting on the back bumper of one of the ambulances, covered in a blanket and sipping a cup of coffee. Beatrice was at his side, holding his arm as the paramedic cut his pants away with a pair if scissors.

"Nasty cut there, Sam. About eight stitches, I'd say," the paramedic remarked.

"A bullet did that?" Captain Boldery asked.

"No, my clumsiness did that," Sam replied. "That damned ice is hard! What are you doing here, boss?"

"I was on my way home when the 'Officer Down' came over the radio. I was afraid it might be you when I heard the street address. I'm told the DOA matches the description from the 7-11 clerk?"

"Yeah. Has to be him. I wounded the other one, too, but he was still able to run."

"We'll warn the hospitals and clinics to be on the lookout. You want some time… take a few days off?"

"Hell no! I've got a feeling I need to act fast."

"What are you going to do?"

"I've got an idea. Tell you about it tomorrow, boss."

"Okay… get that leg taken care of."

"I'm going to drive him to the hospital, now," Beatrice answered. "He won't let the ambulance take him."

"You got any pull with city hall, Captain?"

"What do you need, Sam?"

"Get somebody to plow my fuckin' driveway open!"

Beatrice helped Sam back to his car. "Stay put. I'll go in and get you another pair of pants," she ordered, and was gone.

He leaned back in the seat and closed his eyes. His knee hurt like hell and he was very frightened. Someone had nearly killed him… and threatened his girl. This was not good.

Beatrice returned with the pants and an envelope. "This was inside the screen door." She handed the manila mailing pouch to Sam.

On the way to the hospital, Sam turned on the interior lights in the car and opened the envelope. There was a note, hastily written.

Gretch… they sent a man to kill me. I got lucky. These copies won't stand up in court. They could have been altered. You need to get the hard drives from their computers. All of them.

Even if the e-mails have been deleted, they will still be on the hard drives.

Good luck. Get them son of a bitches.

There was no need for a signature. Sam retrieved a business card from his wallet and dialed a number.

"Who you calling?" Bebe asked.

"FBI, sweets. The fricken' FBI. We got 'em."

"Hello?"

"George?"

"Yes… who is this?"

"Sam Gretch."

"Sam! How did you get this number? I'm at home!"

"You gave it to me… in the plane, remember?"

"Oh, yeah. What's up?"

"Can you meet me in the emergency room at Brookside Hospital? I need your help."

"Give me thirty minutes."

Sam dialed a second number.

"Sterns residence."

"Gordon, Sam Gretch. Can you meet with me and the FBI at Brookside Hospital?"

"When?"

"Right now."

Chapter 69

Bernard Spoolman, AKA, The General, had been a force for some time in cell block 18 of the Menard State Prison. His massive size alone commanded respect from his fellow prisoners. He had been convicted of murder in a robbery gone wrong… however, he had not been an unusually violent man on the outside. On the inside, his following had been growing, and his presence considered a threat by the leaders of other gangs. So, he was eliminated. At eight o'clock in the morning… during breakfast… he was eliminated.

When Noah was taken back to his cell after his interrogation, the usual chatter of the inmates along the hall was not there. It was strangely quiet, eerie. He knew they were wondering. Did he talk? Is he a traitor?

When the guards were gone, he lay down on his bed and closed his eyes. He was exhausted and scared. Why wouldn't he be scared? A murder… right in front of his eyes… and he was unable to help the authorities or risk being killed himself. What a world this was. What a cesspool!

"Noah? You okay?" Harley asked.

"I didn't say anything… if that's what you mean."

"The boys were worried that you might… "

"Well, I didn't. I probably should have… but I didn't. Please leave me alone for awhile."

"Okay… sure. They came and got your computer. See you for lunch."

Chapter 70

The paramedic was wrong. It took eleven stitches to close the wound. The emergency room doctor finished with the needle work and put a neat bandage on his knee.

"Don't get this wet for a couple of days. How you do that is up to you. Go see your regular doctor in a week. I don't want this to get infected. You may have to walk with a straight leg as well, officer. You want to stand and see?"

"Sure, doc. Let's find out." Sam stood and took a tentative step. The cut was low enough that he could bend his knee with only a little pain. "I think I'll be okay… as long as I don't try to run."

"Okay… then I'm done with you. You can take him home, miss." The doctor pulled back the curtains and left the cubical.

Agent George Dirkson was standing in the hallway, a little smirk on his face.

"The nurse at the desk said you busted your knee open on the ice. You need an FBI man for that?"

"Yeah… I want a thorough investigation to find out who put that fricken ice there. Hi George. We gotta talk. Gordon Sterns will be here in a minute.

It was nearly one o'clock before he slipped into the bath Bebe had drawn. The leaf to the dining room table was strategically placed over the tub for him to rest his bandaged leg on.

"What a sight this must be!" he murmured, enjoying the warm water.

Bebe sat on the side of the tub. "I put too much bubble bath in… I can't see your *tallywhacker,*" She said, smiling.

"My *tallywhacker* is just fine! My knee is the problem."

"Oh yeah? Lets see." Bebe found his *tallywhacker* and begin to stoke. The response was immediate. "You're right! It still works!"

"Hmm, that feels good. Don't stop."

She didn't.

Chapter 71

At eight o'clock the next morning, FBI agents along with special investigators from the Illinois State Police, armed with search warrants signed by a federal judge, raided the offices of Orville Merrell, Phillip Augustine, Preston Broderick and Helen Pritchard. At each location, all computers were confiscated and taken to the FBI Crime Lab in Chicago.

It was all there; four different e-mails discussing the assassination of John Pritchard and Arthur Frost… when the need arose. An assassin had been hired and was prepared to act when ordered. The originator of the plan was Orville Merrell himself.

In language that almost everyone in the world will understand… the shit hit the fan. Arrests were made, conspiracy charges were filed, bonds were set, attorneys were hired, and at the recommendation of the FBI, Gordon Sterns was named as first chair prosecuting attorney. The State Attorney wisely decided to schedule a vacation in Italy. Charges were also filed for the murder of Avery Bruin, Linda Ross and the attempted murder of Sam Gretch and Beatrice Martin and Lawrence Coverett, naming Orville Merrell as a conspirator.

Bail had been set for one million dollars for each defendant. By the time the six o'clock news aired the next day, all were out on bail. It helps to be wealthy.

Chapter 72

Captain Boldery called Sam into his office and shut the door. "How's the leg?"

"Hurts like hell," Sam admitted.

"You did a good job, Sam. A very good job." Boldery paused. "I just came back from the Chief's office."

"And…?"

"He's going to make a statement to the press this afternoon. He wants you to be there."

"Do I have to be?"

"Yes, you do. But you won't be talking. He'll do it all. I need to warn you that what he says will not be what happened. He will make it seem like he was in on this from the beginning… that it was all his plan. Oh, he will make you look good… just not as good as himself. You understand what I'm saying?"

"Yes. I understand. What about you?"

"I doubt I'll be mentioned. That's fine with me."

"Okay… thanks for the heads up. That's it?"

"I guess so."

Sam stood. "Well, I got other work to do." *Like finding out why you don't want me poking around in my cold case*, he thought as he left the office.

Chapter 73

It took Robbie nearly a half an hour to tell Noah about the scandal and all the arrests. "Man… can you believe it? In a town like Elmhurst?"

Noah shook his head in dismay. "One of those people had to be responsible for Pritchard's death. And, I'm in here paying for it."

"I brought you the papers so you can read about it." Robbie handed him a bundle of newspapers. "You heard anything from the publisher?" He changed the subject.

"No, not yet. Probably won't. Same ol' same ol'."

"Are you writing another story?"

"I was. My computer privileges have been suspended for awhile."

"For what?"

"They think I witnessed a murder."

"A murder! Did you?"

"No, I didn't see anything. Well, I didn't see who did it, anyway." He knew their conversation was being taped and recorded. "You know me… I'm always looking in the wrong direction."

Then Robbie knew. His brother had seen exactly what had happened. He was never looking in the wrong direction.

"Yeah, well… it's just as well you didn't see it."

"You got that right."

"Well, bro, if you hear anything about getting your book published, let me know."

Chapter 74

A week had passed since the raid. Elmhurst, as well as the entire Chicago-land was abuzz! All the principals named had been indicted for Conspiracy to Commit Murder.

Mayor Augustine resigned immediately, handing over the reigns of the city to his deputy mayor, Pete Brenan. The Elmhurst State Bank board of directors asked for and received Broderick Preston's resignation, as well. Orville Merrell's law license was suspended, pending the outcome of the charges; however, other members of his firm were still allowed to continue to practice law. And Noah Ross was still in prison for a murder he didn't commit.

Later that afternoon, a guard returned Noah's computer.

Well, how about that! I guess I convinced the warden I was telling the truth. "Thank you, officer. I was worried I'd never see this again."

"No problem, scumbag. I'd do the same for any murderer." He spit on the floor at Noah's feet before leaving.

"That's a good sign, Noah," Harley said softly. "You did good. The boys will feel safe, now."

"Well, good for the boys," Noah answered bitterly, as he plugged in the computer. When he turned on the power, he was surprised. There was a message on the screen:

Mr. Ross. I have read several of your stories. They are good, I must admit. I have attempted to write my memoirs of my tenure here as warden. To be frank, my attempts seem rather amateurish compared to yours. Therefore, I will require your help, anonymously, of course. I'll send for you when I am ready.

"Great! Just friggin' great!" Noah muttered.
"What's that?"
"Nothing, Harley. Nothing at all."

The letter came on Friday and was short and to the point:

Mr. Ross,
We have read you manuscript with keen interest and find your story and writing style fresh and your characters compelling. We will be sending you a contract for your consideration. If you find the terms favorable, please sign and return it as soon as possible. Since this is your first publication, we are sorry there is not a lot of room for negotiations. However, we have tried to be fair. If your first attempt proves to be successful, we will open up your next contract to extended negotiations.

Yours truly,
Robert Trenton,
Submission Editor,
Pelican Press.

Noah read the letter for a third time before carefully folding it and putting it in the space reserved for batteries in his computer. *I'm not going to believe it... just yet. Not yet.*

Chapter 75

Sam was sitting at his desk wishing he was somewhere else. He glanced at the clock on the wall. Nine fifteen. His knee was throbbing.

"Sam… we just got a call from a clinic over on Cicero Avenue. A Hispanic guy just checked in with an infected shoulder wound. The intern there says it looks like a gunshot. He read our APB and called. He is stalling the man until we get there." Captain Boldery was pulling on his jacket as he headed for the door. Sam jumped up and followed best he could, limping slightly on his injured leg.

"You going on this one, boss?"

"Yeah. We may need somebody that can run."

"And… that would be …who?"

"Come on, smartass. Let's go get us another bad guy."

The arrest was simple… the easiest one Sam had ever experienced. That was because the fast thinking doctor had given the suspect a double shot of pain killer… which promptly put him to sleep… or so Sam thought.

"He's in there." The doctor pointed behind a curtain.

Sam drew his weapon and Boldery jerked the curtain back.

"You won't need your gun," the doctor said, smiling.

The man was lying on an examining table… snoring loudly.

"Thank you, doctor… you did real good!" Sam said, and then quickly handcuffed the sleeping suspect to the gurney.

"I just followed the instructions of Captain Boldery."

"You told him to put this guy to sleep?" The question was directed at his boss.

"I just thought it would make things easier. Sam, why don't you go on home… rest that knee? I'll take this guy in when he wakes up."

"Does he need to be hospitalized, doctor?" Sam asked.

"No, but someone will have to change that dressing in a couple of days. I shot him full of antibiotics as well."

"Okay then, boss… I'll see you later. My leg is hurting a little." Sam turned and left. *It was always good to have a day off. It was also a little unusual for his boss to take over. Oh, well.*

Sam called Bebe on his way to Garland's. "Hey girlfriend… got time to buy me lunch? I got the rest of the day off."

"Sure… you at Garland's?"

"Will be shortly."

"I can't be there till eleven. Okay?"

"See you then, kiddo."

He slid onto the stool. Looking up at the TV just as WGN broke in with a news flash.

There's been a shooting in the Brookside Clinic parking lot in South Cicero involving an Elmhurst policeman. Early reports indicated a suspect just arrested on a warrant for murdering another policeman earlier this month was attacking the arresting officer when shots were fired. The suspect ap-

pears to have been killed. We will have more information as it becomes available."

Sam was in shock. He tried to call Boldery on his cell, but there was no answer.

"Son of a bitch!"

"What's up?" Jake asked.

"My boss… looks like he killed our only witness involved in Jimmy Frost's murder."

"Bummer."

"Yeah… bummer is right!"

Alverez Cortez never made it to booking. Like his brother three days earlier, he was to die at the hand of a policeman. Captain Boldery's voice seemed frantic when he called dispatch for help.

"The suspect I was bringing in made a lunge at me in the parking lot. He tried to take my gun. I had to shoot him to protect myself." He yelled into the mike. "Send back-up and an ambulance immediately!"

Chapter 76

Noah Ross had placed a call to Beatrice Martin, asking her to come see him at the prison. She did, the very next day.

"How you doing, Noah? You still okay?"

"Yeah, great," he replied bitterly. "I do have something positive to talk to you about, though."

"Good! What's up?"

He handed over the letter from the publisher.

"Oh, wow! This is good news!" she said, genuinely excited.

"You have to promise me you won't tell anybody about this… until we know for sure. Not Detective Gretch nor Robbie… no one."

"Of course. What do you want me to do?"

"You're my attorney… negotiate for me. Get me the best deal you can. Handle all the details. I am rather restricted in here."

"Well, of course… the firm will be happy to represent you. But, I don't think it should be me. Amber Street is our litigation expert. She would be more suitable to handle this for you. If that is all right?"

"Yes… as long as she understands… no one is to know about this until I am ready. Do I know her?"

"No, she joined the firm after… after your trial."

"I see."

Beatrice smiled. "Wow… I'm impressed. A real live author! I'm sitting across from a real live author!"

Noah smiled back. "Don't get too excited… I am still in prison, remember?" It was hard for him to hide his excitement.

"You should never have sent me home, Captain!" Sam stated angrily. They were in Boldery's office. "Now we got nothing… no witnesses... nothing. I thought you were smarter than that! That was stupid!" Sam Gretch was pissed.

"Watch it, smartass. I'm the boss remember."

"Did you have to kill the guy?"

"That's enough… get the hell out of here while you still got a job."

Sam turned and walked out, slamming the door hard as he went. *How could an experienced police officer have botched this up?*

Chapter 77

Three Months Later

Helen Pritchard, on the advice of her new attorney, agreed to testify against the others in return for special consideration from the Prosecuting Attorney. Preston Broderick, the honorable Mayor Augustine, and the renowned lawyer, Orville Merrell, were all going away for a long time, or so thought most. The evidence from the confiscated computers was so overwhelming that the trial, presided over by a judge named Trundle, lasted only eight days. Sentencing followed quickly and that's when the surprise bomb exploded. Orville Merrill, Preston Broderick and the mayor each received the minimum sentence of eight years, eligible for parole after only four, incarnation to be at the minimum security facility in Joliet. Helen Pritchard was sentenced to five years probation. Gordon Sterns earned a lot of recognition for his efforts at the trial, and nobody was more surprised at the light sentences than he.

"What the hell just happened," Sam asked Sterns as the reporters were racing from the courtroom to file their stories.

"Looks like somebody got paid a lot of money. This is an embarrassment! My office will investigate this. Good Lord, what a joke!"

Chapter 78

A year had passed since the murder of John Pritchard. Noah was getting used to prison life; and Sam Gretch was still trying to make sense of the note left in Pritchard's robe pocket. He and Bebe were getting even closer to being a permanent thing and Robbie... Robbie was still Robbie.

It was the middle of April and he had just come back from an early Saturday morning fishing jaunt. Dropping clothes as he went, he grabbed a beer from the fridge, and headed for the shower. The water felt good, and he finished the beer standing in the spray, thinking about his secret. After he dried, he slipped on a pair of baggy underwear and headed to the couch for the afternoon game, fetching another beer as he passed through the kitchen. He was just ready to flop down when he noticed the car coming up the lane. It was black and long and very clean.

Who in the hell is that? he asked himself.

The car pulled to a stop in the drive and the door opened. A pair of nylon encased legs appeared, followed by the stylish figure of a very attractive, middle aged woman.

Holy shit...what is she doing here?

He answered the gentle knock on the door, hiding most of his scantily clad body behind the open door.

"Yes, ma'am, may I help you?"

"Mr. Ross. Do you remember who I am?"

"Yes, ma'am... Mrs. Pritchard. I do remember you, of course."

"May I come in?"

She had on a short, black skirt that most women her age would have looked ridiculous in and a light cashmere sweater, the top four buttons unfastened. Robbie stood to the side, and let her enter, noticing that the upper portion of her breasts shook like vanilla Jell-O when she walked.

No bra, he thought. He stood awkwardly, his hands cupped over the front of his shorts just incase the fly was open. If she noticed the mess the room was in, she never let on.

"How have you been, Mr. Ross?"

Robbie was embarrassed. "Nobody ever calls me Mr. Ross. Can I get you a beer? No, of course not... I'm sorry," he mumbled. "I don't have any wine."

"No, thank you. I came here to apologize for getting you in trouble... back when John was killed. I'm sorry for that."

"You didn't get me in trouble. You don't need to apologize." He paused, still not in control. "I'm sorry the place is a mess. I just got out of the shower."

"I can see that." She reached a hand and caressed his cheek. "Your hair is still wet."

He shivered.

"You are a very handsome boy... even more so than I remembered... and even more so without clothes." Her touch went down from his cheek and caressed his chest. "I'm not sure why I'm here... Robbie. May I call you Robbie? I have been thinking about you a lot lately. It gets lonely in the house."

"Mrs. Pritchard... this is not a good idea."

"Why not, Robbie. You have something else to do?"

"No, ma-am. But… "

"You're so young," she panted.

"Mrs. Pritchard…. I don't… "

Her hand traveled downward and Robbie's head went back, his eyes staring at the ceiling beam.

"Good grief," he said quietly.

Twenty minutes later, she buttoned the cashmere sweater all the way to the top, picked up her lavender panties, which she put in her purse, and faced the naked Robbie sprawled out on the couch.

"You weren't as good as I anticipated. I had hoped for more."

Robbie smiled. "I thought it was great." He decided to end this right away. "I never fucked a grandma before."

She turned on her heel and stormed out the door.

"Crazy broad," he muttered, looking at the torn magazines on the coffee table. "Why do they always want to do it on the table?" He smoothed out the wrinkles on Miss April as the long black car went sailing back down the lane.

Chapter 79

"You're not going to believe who came out to the cabin yesterday." Robbie was sitting in the steel chair in the cold room at Menard Prison.

"You do like to play games, don't you? So, tell me… who came out to your cabin yesterday?"

"Helen Pritchard."

Noah's eyes shot up. "Really? What the hell for?"

"She wanted to get screwed. So, I screwed her."

"You're kidding me, right?"

"Nope. Poked her on the coffee table. Got gooey shit all over my Playboys."

"No way!"

"Way! She said I wasn't all that good, which pissed me off, so I pissed her off. She won't be back."

"You are something else, brother."

"Yeah, well, there you go. I'll take that as a compliment.' He grinned. "I think she's the oldest woman I ever poked!"

Noah could think of nothing to say… so he just smiled and shook his head in wonder.

Three days later Noah got another visitor.

"You're getting' as popular as Oprah," the guard grinned, opening up the cell door. "Don't mind takin' you ta this one, tho… this one's a looker!" Gruner was one of the more likable guards. He had two brothers in prison, so he had a little empathy.

Noah wasn't expecting anyone. Certainly not the black-haired beauty in the dark blue pinstripe business suit, waiting in the uncomfortable steel chair.

"Hi, Mr. Ross. I'm Amber Street. Ms. Martin thought we ought to meet." She stood and offered her hand. "This is the first time I have ever been a prison. Not too cool, huh?"

He was, as they say, thunderstruck. "You're Mrs. Street?" he blurted, sure he sounded like an idiot. He had had an image of a matronly, middle-aged woman wearing brown box-like shoes.

"No… not Mrs… Miss. Miss Street. I'm not married."

"I see…" he responded, still in a trance.

"I've talked to your publisher's submission editor, and managed to get you a modest advance and an increase of your royalties from 8 to 12 percent. I should have a proof of the cover design for you to look at in a week or so. If it meets with your approval, another few weeks and we should have a proof of the complete book. I've brought the contract for you to sign." She took a blue legal folder from her soft-sided briefcase.

This was too much for Noah. "You… you've done all this already?"

"Ms. Martin said you were anxious… that you have been trying to get a book published for several years. Besides, it was fun. I read the manuscript. I hope you don't mind."

Her eyes were sea foam green… with dark, full lashes that framed them like an expensive oil painting.

"What did you think?" he asked. Suddenly, it was important to him for her to like it.

"I thought it was wonderful. I can't believe you haven't been published before."

"Amber Street," he stated softly. "What a wonderful name. Where did you come from?"

"Cincinnati, originally. I've been in Chicago for three years now, but I'm moving to Elmhurst as soon as I can find an apartment."

Noah could not take his eyes from her face. "I'm sure this is not appropriate… I've been in here for some time now which might have affected me… but you are the most attractive woman I have ever met," he stammered. She said nothing, but searched his face for… perhaps sincerity. He felt compelled to add, "I'm sorry. That was out of line. Certainly not professional." Her smile was soft and forgiving. He had done nothing wrong.

"Beatrice says you're innocent. The manuscript says you're innocent. I hope that's true, Noah Ross. I have a feeling I'm going to be helping her and her friend the cop to get you out of here."

"That would be… that would be real nice."

Chapter 80

It was a Saturday morning and Sam had cooked a breakfast of scrambled eggs with green and red peppers, made a pot of coffee, poured two glasses of orange juice and headed back to the bedroom with the heavy laden tray. Beatrice had stashed three pillows behind her head and was sitting up against the headboard, the sheet covering most of her bare breasts.

"You get more beautiful every day," Sam said softly, setting the tray on the night stand.

"Oh, you nice man… that looks fantastic.! Just for that… you get a look." She slid the sheet down, exposing the rest of her soft things, then quickly pulled it back in place. "More after I eat," she promised.

Sam laughed. "That sounds like a plan."

Later that morning, they made a Wal-mart run. Sam bought some socks and underwear and Beatrice bought a barrage of bottles and tubes from the beauty and health care section. Sam's bill came to $14.45. Beatrice's bill came to $88.28. They were walking to the car in the parking lot.

"Damn! Glad I don't have to buy all that stuff to stay beautiful!" he teased.

"When were you ever beautiful?" she came back.

"You are in trouble, young lady"

They returned home and were putting things away when the phone rang. "I'll get it," Sam announced, picking up the receiver.

"Sam, Jake Garland. Listen, I was going through my safe last night and came across an envelope that Jimmy Frost gave me three or four months ago. To tell you the truth, I had forgotten all about it. Anyway… it's for you. I remember when he gave it to me, he told me to give it to you if anything ever happened to him. I'm sorry I forgot."

"No problem, Jake. Any idea what's in it?"

"No… he didn't say and I never asked."

"Okay. We'll probably be in sometime today. Thanks." He stared at the phone for a minute before hanging up.

"What?" Beatrice asked.

"Jimmy Frost left an envelope for me at Garland's… three or four months ago. Jake said he made him promise to give it to me if anything ever happened to him. We should go there for lunch."

Chapter 81

Sam Gretch was anxious to get to Garland's. A mysterious envelope… from his best friend… his best friend that was murdered, and an envelope not to be delivered unless something bad happened.

They took their usual back booth and ordered beers. Jake brought the glasses along with a business size sealed envelope. A single word was on the outside. "Sam".

His hands shook as he opened it up, careful not to damage the contents. The letter was dated May 2, 2003. Four days after he had made homicide detective.

"Sam,

If you're reading this, then it's probably because somebody popped my cork. That has been a concern of mine for some time now. Anyway, there are some things you need to know.

An incident happened... two years before you joined the force. I was on the job only three months and as green as they get, cruisin' the three to midnight shift. The first two or three months are the worst, you know. Always scared of getting shot or having a wreck. Anyway, I get this call... shots fired in the parking lot of Murphy's Motel. I damned near shit in my pants as I was driving over there.

When I arrived on the scene, was I surprised. Frank Boldery was already there. He was a lieutenant back then. He said he was in the neighborhood and heard the call come over the radio. I found out later that couldn't be true. He was in his personal car... and there was no radio in it.

There was a body in the hedge next to the parking lot. The man was obviously dead... with a huge hole in the back of his head. According to his driver's license, his name was Donald Anderson.

Boldery took charge, which I was very thankful for at the time, since I had no idea what to do first. He said he would take care of the investigation. But, he didn't. Investigate, I mean. He never talked to anyone at the motel or in the neighborhood. He also told me he would take care of all the paper work. Fine with me. I didn't know what to do anyway, right?

The next day, Boldery comes to see me at my apartment. Starts talking about how us cops should always stick together, watch each other's back and so forth. Wanted to make sure he could count on me to do the right thing. He said that I shouldn't rattle the bushes about the Anderson case. If anybody asked about it, I was to get really dumb. Then he said something about making my life miserable, or worse, if I didn't keep my nose out of it.

When I found out he didn't have a police radio in his car, I really got suspicious. But... like I said, I was young, and I was afraid of what he could do to me. So, all these years I've kept quiet. Then you made homicide detective and, of all things, pulled out the cold case on Donald Anderson.
Bottom line is... I couldn't prove anything then, and I sure as hell can't prove anything now, but if I was betting... I'd give you a hundred to one that Boldery killed Anderson. Rumor had it Anderson was poking Boldery's wife and he caught them coming out of the motel that night. They were divorced right after that and she moved away.
I know I should have come forward a long time ago. But the past is the past. I can't change that. Now, the ball is in your court, friend. Go get him.

Jimmy

Slowly, he folded the letter and looked into Beatrice's face. His mind was whirling… things were starting to make more sense.

"What?" she asked.

"Another airplane fell out of the sky. Only this time, its hit Boldery on the head."

He read the letter to her.

Chapter 82

Frank Boldery had spent the last two hours firing his forty-four at the black silhouettes which represented the bad guys. He had killed every one that he shot at. He put his gun back in the holster, and walked out of the firing range and into the sunlight of the early Saturday afternoon. He drove to a fast food restaurant, got a hamburger and drink, then drove to Hawk Hollow Forrest Preserve and parked in a remote area.

"Got to think," he muttered, taking a bite of his sandwich. Sam Gretch was not going to let up. The Cortez brothers had done only half the job by taking out Jimmy Frost. The botched attempt on Sam had left him no choice but to eliminate the witness. He was sure the remaining brother would have given him up in an instant. That bit of action made Sam Gretch even more suspicious, he realized. None the less, it had to be done. Now… how to get rid of Sam without implicating himself? That would not be easy. He knew Sam was on full alert, and Orville Merrell was no longer available to help.

His hands began to shake and his stomach heaved. Was it was finally over? Were they going to find out the truth? Yes, Gretch was going to get him. Sweat broke out on his forehead. Realization was setting in. He knew he had no choice. Suddenly, he knew what he had to do. "I hope you will enjoy this, Gretch. You bastard!"

His cell phone rang, interrupting his thoughts.

"Boldery."

"Where are you?"
"Hawk Hollow Forest Preserve… having lunch."
"Perfect. Stay there. I'll be there in about twenty minutes. We have to talk."
"Yes. We certainly do."

Chapter 83

Monday

It had been awhile since Sam had been in the basement. Mulvaney was not in his office.

"Damn it, I need to talk to you, Joe," he muttered, returning back to the upper floor and his desk. He didn't want to leave a note on the door, not knowing who else might read it. He tried to do some paperwork, but couldn't concentrate, so he decided to go find Joe Mulvaney. He was changing light bulbs in the courtroom.

"So, there you are, my information wizard. I need you."

"Uh oh! Tracked me down. Must be really important. Hand me that bulb, will you, Sam?" The maintenance guru was standing on a ladder. He replaced the burnt out bulb and descended. "What's on your feeble mind, Sam?"

"Boldery. What do you know about Boldery?"

"Well, now. Captain Boldery, is it? May I remind you he is your superior and out-ranks me by at least twenty levels."

"I know who he is. What do you know about him?"

"Oh, my. Well, I know, from my many years as a janitor, that when you discover a bunch of cockroaches, when you exterminate them… you rarely get them all."

"Are you saying Boldery is a cockroach?"

"One of them… but he's not the only one around." He leaned the ladder against the wall. "How would you like to buy me a cup of coffee? It's time for my break."

Sam was perplexed. Mulvaney had given him more that he had expected. A lesson in cockroaches, indeed. Well, first things first.

He placed a call to information and asked for the number of Loretta Boldery. Mulvaney had told him the rumor was that she had moved to Indianapolis soon after the divorce was final. There was no such person listed there.

Next, he called the Bureau of Records for Cook County. Here he was told Loretta Boldery's maiden name was Shanney. Armed with that information, he called the Bureau of Records for Indianapolis. He wasn't expecting the results he got.

A Ms. Loretta Shanney died on September 20, 1994. The cause of death was listed as a homicide… a gunshot wound to the head. There was no additional information, so said the clerk. Talk about the tip of the iceberg. He called the Indianapolis Police Department.

"Homicide, Parker."

"Officer, I'm Detective Sam Gretch, Elmhurst, Illinois. I'm working a cold case here that may have some bearing on one of your cold cases. Are you the guy I need to talk to?"

"I've been around quite awhile. How can I help you, detective?"

"Do you remember a woman named Loretta Shanney? She was murdered in Indy in 1994."

"Shanney? Yes, I do remember the case. It's been awhile since I've looked at the file, though. If I remember right, she was getting into her car when she was shot and robbed."

"Robbed? So, he tried to make it look like a robbery. I think it's possible the killer is here… in Elmhurst."

"Really? And who would that be?"

"A fellow policeman." He decided to be blunt.

Parker's interest went up considerably. "Listen, why don't I drive up and see you? Maybe we can help each other solve a couple of old ones. Besides, I'm always looking for an excuse to get out of town."

"That would be fine with me."

"Great. Why don't I come up tomorrow afternoon? I'll bring my evidence box."

"I'll look forward to seeing you."

"Any good restaurants there?"

Don Parker took the trip request into his boss for a signature.

"Why are you going to Chicago?"

"Cold case. Officer there thinks he knows who killed this girl." He slid the file over to his boss.

"Oh, I remember this."

"The cop in Elmhurst thinks it could be one of his fellow policemen. I need to check it out."

"A bad cop? Yeah, okay. Stay out of trouble. Chicago is a big place." He signed the request.

Gordon Sterns was in Springfield attending a conference titled *The law and Politics* being held in the state capitol building. A conference aide gave him the note which read, *Call Sam Gretch at once. Utmost importance*.

Perturbed, he left the room as quietly as possible and made his way to the lobby where he called Sam on his cell phone.

"This better be good, Sam. What the hell's going on?" For the next five minutes, he listened intently as Sam explained what he had learned about Boldery.

"Sam, I'll be back in Chicago tomorrow. Don't do anything until I get there. I mean it, damn it… don't do anything! I'll have to get Internal Affairs involved."

Chapter 84

Tuesday

Captain Boldery had not been in his office since Friday. It was not easy for Sam to accept that his boss was a murderer. And what was he going to do about that? Could he prove anything? *Come on Sterns, call me!*

"Anybody know where Boldery is?" he addressed the group.

Nobody knew. Nobody cared.

Don Parker arrived at the station around three o'clock. Sam took him and both their files into an interview room and locked the door. For the next two hours, the two men compared cases. There were striking similarities. Both victims had been killed in a parking lot. Both had been shot at close range in the back of the head. Both had been shot with the same type of weapon… most likely a forty-four magnum. The most significant evidence was… a shell casing found at the scene in Indianapolis.

"So, you think it's your boss. Let's bring him in here and sweat him a little. Maybe he'll give it up."

"I think I'd better wait for the State's Attorney," Sam answered. "He should be here sometime today. He said something about Cook County Internal Affairs handling it. Any way, I don't know where my boss is."

"You talked to the State Attorney?"

"Yesterday. He was out of town. Said he'd be back today."

"Shit... that means they'll take over... we get no fun. By the way, why would your guy kill somebody in Indianapolis, anyway? "

"It was his ex-wife."

"Ex-wife? I don't think so. My vic was never married... born and raised in Indy."

"No way! Really?"

"Yep. You got the wrong Loretta Shanney."

Sam's heart sank. "I thought I had him nailed," he muttered. " I guess you made a wasted trip."

Parker was not so affected. "Listen, I'm on an expense book! Where's the best place to get a steak in Chicago? No use to make my trip a total waste."

"Well, I don't know about the best, but I personally like Harry Caray's Steak House."

"The baseball announcer?"

"Yep."

"Lead the way brother. I'm buying!"

Sam tried to hide his disappointment. "Let me make a call first. Keep peace in the family, so to speak."

"You married?" Parker asked, surprised. "I didn't think any homicide cops were married. Not for long, anyway."

"Yeah, you're right about that. But I do have a girl. A great girl. She lives with me."

"I've got several girl friends... but none of them would enjoy living with me!" Parker laughed.

Sam dialed Bebe's direct number.

"Talk to me, Sam," she said. "I have three minutes." Welcome to caller I.D.

"Bebe, I'm going to take Detective Parker to Harry Caray's for dinner. Probably be home late. Didn't want you to worry."

"That's fine, Sam. I have plans that involve a glass of wine and a book tonight. Now, I'll be able to use your recliner. Be careful and have a good time."

"Thanks, hon. I'll be careful. By the way, the Indianapolis thing didn't work out. I'm back to square one with Boldery."

"Oh… too bad. I'm sorry."

"Yeah, me to. See you later."He hung up.

"She okay with that?" Parker asked.

"Yeah… she's excited because she gets to sit in my chair."

"I'll never understand women."

Chapter 85

Gordon Sterns was late getting back to Chicago. He had been approached by a rather influential group and asked to run for State's Attorney in the next election. After several hours of discussion, he decided he would do just that. He shouldn't have any problem defeating his boss. Especially with this new backing.

He called the head of the Internal Affairs Office of the Illinois State Police and officially requested an investigation into the allegations presented by Sam Gretch into the actions of Captain Frank Boldery. As always, the gang of sharp-toothed sharks were only too happy to oblige. There was something about the smell of blood, particularly when it was from one of their own.

Calls to Sam's office phone went unanswered. *Probably out catching more bad guys,* he thought.

The restaurant was fun, as usual, and the food was great. A couple of the Chicago Cub players were having a few drinks at the bar and Parker was able to get their autographs. He was like a kid at a party. Sam went easy on the booze, not wanting to get a DUI on the way home. Parker, on the other hand, knowing he was in good hands, had several vodka martinis and as they say, was shit-faced by the time they left for home. Sam dropped his new temporary partner at his hotel in Elmhurst just after eleven. He would be home in five minutes.

His first reaction was one of immense fear. All the lights were on in the apartment and the front door was standing wide open. His hands trembled as he pulled his weapon and slowly crept up the porch stairs.

"Bebe? You there?" he asked loudly.

No answer. He readied his gun and stepped into the living room.

"Anyone here?" he asked again. Silence.

A partially filled glass of wine was on the end table by his chair. An open book was lying next to the glass. A coverlet was tossed carelessly on the chair arm. He saw her purse on the stand by the front door, her car keys lying next to it. Everything was there as it should be. Everything... except Bebe.

A search of the apartment produced nothing. She was gone. Panic was about to overtake him when he heard a noise on the porch. He drew his weapon and crouched, pointing the gun at the open doorway. Bebe appeared, holding something furry in her arms. She discovered Sam aiming the gun at her and she screamed, dropping the furry thing on the floor and covering her face with her hands."

Quickly, Sam lowered his gun. "Bebe! You okay?"

"My God, you scared the hell out of me? Where did she go?"

"Where did who go?"

"The cat! Where did the cat go?"

"That was a cat? It went that way." Sam pointed toward the kitchen. "What in the hell is going on? I thought you had been kidnapped!"

"Kidnapped? You've been watching too many bad movies. I was reading my book, and I kept hearing this noise... sounded like a baby crying. So

I went outside to check and I found the cat sitting on the window sill. When I tried to grab her, she ran up the street. I could see she was hurt, so I went after her. I caught her at the corner. I think she's been hit by a car. Her back leg is skinned up bad. Anyway, I was bringing her back here when I saw you go in the house. The rest you know. I need to get her to a vet."

Sam returned his gun to the holster and collapsed on the couch, hoping his breathing would soon return to normal.

"A cat. An injured cat. What the hell 's next?"

Don Parker decided to have one more drink before going to his room. The lounge was nearly empty and he had no problem finding a vacant stool at the bar. He staggered a little, but managed to perch his large frame on the seat on the second try.

"What can I get you?" The bartender was young, kinda cute, but obviously had a lot of miles on her. The skin on her face was not nearly as smooth as the skin on the exposed part of her large breasts.

"A woman… that can understand me." He belched. "Excuse me. That just slipped out. I'll have a vodka martini. Go easy on the martini part."

"Are you staying in the hotel?" she asked.

"Yes. You want my room number, don't you?" he smiled.

She smiled back. "No, I just wasn't going to serve you if you were driving. If you're staying here, then okay… you can get as drunk as you want."

"Oh, I see." He burped again. "So, you don't want my body?"

"Well, I do… but I have great self-control over my temptations. Also, there's a chance I *would* understand you… and that would be disastrous." She sat the drink in front of him.

"You're right. Absolutely disastrous!" he slurred, downing the drink in one gulp and then promptly fell off the stool, flat on his back.

Chapter 86

They found the cat hiding under the kitchen table. It was shivering from fright and Sam noticed a bloody patch of skin on her rear leg.

"She's been hurt. Probably a car."

"I said that."

Beatrice got down on all fours and gently took her into her arms. "Poor thing," she whined, petting her tenderly behind the ears. "I'll take her to the vet's in the morning."

"Good idea. I think she'll be alright till then."

Don Parker was dreaming that a woman was on top of him and rocking back and forth. He could smell stale cigarette smoke and his mouth was as dry as a handful of hay. The dream was so real.

"Come on, honey. Wake up and enjoy this." The voice was soft and definitely female. "Oh, that's good!"

He opened one eye, however, not without considerable effort. She was naked, her breasts swinging to and fro in time with her rocking. The sight was enough to encourage him to open his other eye.

"Oh, there you are," she panted. "'Bout time you joined this party."

"That feels really good," he managed. "You have any trouble getting' it up?"

"Not a bit. When I woke up… there it was standing… like a flag pole. I decided not… to waste it. Oh, yes!" She shut her eyes and began to shudder. Obviously, she had reached the end of her goal.

He let himself surrender to the ecstasy of the moment and quickly joined her to the finish. She collapsed on his chest, smashing her softness into his flesh. The cigarette smell was almost more than his hangover could handle.

"Where are we?" he asked.

"Your hotel room."

"How did *we* get here?"

"You passed out in the bar. I saw the gun and the badge. I never done a policeman before. So, I had the night man help me get you to your room, and decided to stay. When I woke up… you were sticking up like a pecker-head mushroom. The rest you know."

"I feel like hell."

She rolled off his chest, sat on the side of the bed, and lit a cigarette. "You want one?"

"No. Don't use 'em. Can't stand them, really."

"Oh, one of those guys, huh?"

"Yeah, that's me. I wish you'd put it out."

She stood up. "Screw you. Oh, I guess I just did, didn't I?"

He decided she didn't look nearly as pretty when he was sober. "Yeah, thanks. You can go now." He really felt like shit. "Your tits are all wrinkled."

She grabbed her clothes and went into the bathroom. In a minute she came out, went straight to the door and left without another word.

Man, I hope she was clean, he thought.

He made coffee in the little pot, showered and dressed, then called Sam's number at the station. A glance at his watch notified him it was 9:17.

"Homicide, Gretch."

"Sam… Parker. I was going to buy you breakfast. Sorry, buddy, I just woke up. We had quite a night. It was fun. Thanks again."

"No problem, Parker. Thanks for coming up. Take care."

He hung up the phone which rang immediately.

"Gretch."

"Dispatch, Sam… we got a call from the Forest Preserve Office. They found Captain Boldery's car at Hawk Hollow Forest Preserve. They say there is a dead man in the front seat and his brains are all over the side window. We got two black and whites on the way, but I thought you'd want to go.

Chapter 87

When Sam arrived, there were five police cars already there. One of the uniforms who he knew casually approached him as he got out of the car.

"What have you got, George?"

"Look's like he shot himself, Sam. He's been here for a few days."

"You move anything?"

"No, just opened the door. I called the lab boys."

Sam looked in the car. "Christ! Anything else?"

"No, not on the surface. The guard here said they were off duty on the weekend, so he could have been here since Friday."

The Captain's gun was on the floor by the accelerator pedal. A coke cup and a Burger King bag were in the passenger seat. He was slumped over, and whatever was left of his head was resting on the steering wheel.

"George, if you were planning on shooting yourself in the head, would you have a hamburger first?"

"Probably not," he answered.

Sam shook his head in agreement. "Well, at least now we know why he hasn't been to work," he muttered as he walked over to open the back door. A small piece of paper on the floor caught his eye. Carefully, he picked it up by the edges. It was a Tootsie-roll wrapper, neatly folded into a square.

"George, bring me a baggie."

When the lab technicians arrived, Sam handed over the baggie. "Test this for prints. Also, make sure you test the Captain's hand for gunpowder residue. I know it looks like a suicide, but maybe not. Let's be sure."

The small town of Elmhurst was trying to recover from more tragedies in the last three years than in the entire history of the town. It all started with Pritchard's murder, then Noah's conviction, the conspiracy to commit murder by several top citizens of the community, Jimmy Frost's murder, the attempt to kill Sam... and now, the second-ranking officer in the police department found shot to death in his car.

The station was unusually quiet. Everyone was still in shock. The Chief had issued orders that all promotions and transfers would be frozen until a comprehensive investigation of Boldery's death was completed. The State Police and the FBI were to name a task force to work together to help accomplish this.

Sam was not sure what direction to go. It had been two weeks since the captain had been found. He stared at the five inch pile of papers in his in-basket... at lease four days of work to complete the past due reports. *Should I do these today or wait till later... maybe next month... or next year?* The phone interrupted his thoughts. He shifted his stare from the paperwork to the phone but made no move to answer it

When it rang for the fifth time, Artie across the aisle yelled.

"Get the phone, dick head. It won't answer itself!"

"Bite me," Sam returned, but reached and picked up the receiver.

"Gretch," he growled.

"Sam, Don Parker, Indianapolis P.D."

"Parker… how you doing?" Sam was surprised at the call.

"Good, Sam, good. Listen, I think I may have found the woman you thought was my vic. After I got back home, my curiosity was aroused, so I did some checking. There's a Loretta Shanney who moved to Brownsburg about the time we were looking at my homicide. Brownsburg is west of here about ten miles. Anyway, I have her number if you're interested.

"Parker… I love you!"

"Aw, shucks."

Chapter 88

"Ms. Shanney, my name is Detective Gretch from Elmhurst. Sorry to be so blunt, but were you once married to Frank Boldery?"

"That's a long time ago, detective. I'd just as soon forget about that. Frank Boldery was a dirt bag. Why are you calling me?"

"Well, first, I need to tell you that Frank is dead." He paused to let that sink in.

"Well. So he's gone. I haven't thought about him for a long time. I can't say that I'm upset. You said, first. What else?" She was unemotional.

"I'm sorry to be blunt, but I have to ask. Were you having an affair with Donald Anderson back in August of 94, when he was killed?"

"Me? Good Lord, no, it wasn't me. Frank told me about it though. You need to look a little higher up the chain."

Sam was shocked. "Are you sure?"

"Yes. That's all I can say."

"Could Frank have been involved in some way?"

"Well, I don't know. He was in charge of the investigation. Why?"

"A friend of mine… a fellow policeman… thought you were the woman involved and that Frank may have killed Anderson in a fit of rage."

"Frank was not a nice man, detective, but since it wasn't me, he would have no reason to kill anybody."

"Okay, well, sorry I had to tell you about Frank's death. You've been very helpful. Thank you."

"You're welcome, Detective, but Frank ceased to be anybody I cared about a long time ago. Goodbye."

Chapter 89

It had been a slow week for the Elmhurst homicide detective. No murders, not even any shootings… a slow week indeed. Thursday morning he was called into the office of the Chief of Police, Warren Staff, located on the top floor of city hall.

Does he suspect anything? He asked himself. *No, surely not.*

"Sam… come in. Have a seat."

"Thank you, sir."

"Tootsie-roll?"

"No thank you, sir."

The room was void on any sign of work, even though it was after ten. An empty in-box, an empty out-box and no papers whatsoever on the desk. Next to the phone was a large glass bowl of mini Tootsie-rolls.

The computer screen on the credenza was dark. It hadn't been turned on. Next to the dark monitor was a NFL football signed by Gale Sayers.

"I wanted to personally commend you on the job you have done over the past few years. I know it has been rough on you… loosing your best friend and dealing with Boldery's situation." The man was intently filing an already immaculate nail.

How about your situation? he thought. Out loud he said, "Yeah… it's been kinda rough."

"Of course it has. I need to fill the position of captain. You are the most likely candidate. Before I can do that, however, I must have some… assurances."

"I don't understand."

"I think you do. I'm not much of a policeman and you know it. I'm a figurehead. I make great speeches. That's about it. However, I like my job. And, I want to keep it. In other words, the man I pick for captain will have to do his job without any help from me. The only time I get involved is to criticize you if I'm getting heat from the mayor or the town council. When things go wrong, it's your fault. When things go right… I get the credit. Can you work under those conditions?"

"I guess the alternative would be to work for some one not as qualified as myself?"

"Exactly."

"Can I think about that for a day or two? I've been thinking about getting married. I'd like to discuss this with my fiancée."

"Married!" Staff shook his head. "I remember those days. Good riddance!"

"Sir?"

"Can't trust them, Sam. Minute your head is turned, they're bangin' somebody else."

"How long you been divorced, sir?" Sam was fishing.

"Ehh… long time ago. She's in Memphis I think."

"That's too bad, sir."

"Yeah, well, no big deal. You got the weekend. Let me know on Monday."

"Thank you, sir."

"Sam… let's keep this to ourselves as far as the rest of the department is concerned… until you make up your mind."

"Of course."

As he walked back to his desk, his mind was concentrating on a statement Mulvaney had made.

You rarely get all the roaches. Maybe sometimes you do. Maybe this time I will.

He called Beatrice and told her of the job offer.

"Congratulations, Sammie! Way to go."

"Thanks, Bebe. It's not as glamorous as it sounds. I'm not sure I'll take it. There's some strings attached." Suddenly, he was aware of someone standing in front of his desk, He looked up and found Jimmy Frost's father standing there. "I'll call you back in a little while."

"I'm due in court in twenty minutes. Let's talk about it at dinner."

"Okay. See you later." He hung up the receiver. "Mr. Frost… Arthur… how are you?"

"Good, Sam. Very good, for an old fellow." He greeted Sam with a warm smile.

"What brings you here?"

"Oh, I wanted to personally thank you for finding Jimmy's killer. You promised me you would, and you kept your promise."

"You're welcome." Sam smiled. "You didn't need to come down here to tell me that."

"Well, I didn't. I came here to give you something. Would you come with me, please?"

"Where?"

"Just outside. Come, please."

Sam followed the older man outside. At the curb was Jimmy Frost's Ford Bronco… and attached to it was the boat, a twenty-seven foot Stingray named *Precious*.

Sam was speechless, his mouth open in shock.

Arthur frost handed him a set of keys. "Here, Sam. This is all yours now."

"Arthur… no… I can't…"

"Hogwash! You can and you will. "
"I don't know what to say."
"A simple thank you will suffice."

Still in a daze from his recent windfall, Sam returned to his desk and opened the file on Donald Anderson. At least now he didn't have to worry about Boldery raising hell about this cold case. And it had been rather easy to find out where Warren Staff's ex-wife lived.

He picked up the phone. "Memphis Tennessee information, please."

Chapter 90

Beatrice was in the mood for Chinese so they had driven over on Ogden Avenue to a restaurant called Ming's Palace. They had placed their orders and were enjoying a glass of wine.

"So, tell me about this job. Captain sounds like a pretty prestigious title, to me," she kidded.

"There's something else I need to tell you first. Chances are… I'll never be captain. I know who killed Donald Anderson."

"It wasn't Boldery?"

"No, it was not Boldery. He was the cover up, though. If I tell you who Anderson was screwing around with, you'll know who the killer is."

"And that would be?"

He leaned over the table and whispered a name.

Her eyes opened wide. "No… you can't be serious!"

"I called her today."

It was nearly nine when they returned to their apartment. Sam fixed a couple of after-dinner drinks and they sat on the front steps to enjoy the evening.

"So what are you going to do?" she asked.

"I'm going to see Sterns in the morning. See what he says."

"You better be very careful… and very sure before you do anything."

"Don't worry about that. Sterns will probably take over. I'll be out of it."

"Good. That's good." They sipped their drinks for a few minutes, neither saying anything.

"How hard is it to get a private investigator's license?" That question was out of the blue.

"Why?" he asked, cautiously.

"Excuse me for being nosey, but how much did you make last year?"

"Close to fifty thousand." He wasn't necessarily proud of that.

"I paid twice that much to private investigators last year, just for my small firm. There's a big demand out there. I could get you clients galore. I bet you could bring in four hundred thousand or more."

"No… you think?" He had never thought much about money. As long as he could pay the bills… that was enough.

"I think."

"Wow."

"Besides, if you weren't a cop… we could get married."

He choked, spitting his Amaretto across the steps, then he broke into a fit of coughing. Covering his mouth with his hand, it took him a minute to regain control.

"Married?" he asked weakly.

She remained silent, a smile playing around the corner of her lips."

He had been lying to Chief Staff earlier about getting married. Did she somehow know about what he said?

Chapter 91

Three days later, at eight a.m., Gordon Sterns and two state Internal Affairs officers knocked on the open door of the Elmhurst Chief of Police's office and entered, closing the door behind them. Warren Staff looked up from the golf magazine he was reading.

"Gordon. What a nice surprise. What can I do for you?"

"Mr. Staff. Before I continue, I must ask you to hand over your weapon and place your hands on the desk where we can see them."

His face became beet red in an instant. "What the hell is going on here?" he demanded.

"Gun, please. I can have one of my men take it from you if you insist." The taller of the two officers drew his own piece and held it at ready.

Slowly, Warren Staff withdrew his gun from his shoulder holster and laid it on the desk. "You better have a damn good reason for this," he growled.

"How about a murder charge… is that reason enough?" Sterns picked up the gun and handed it to one of his assistants.

"You're crazy. What murder?"

"How about Donald Anderson, for starters? Then probably Frank Boldery. There could even be more. We'll find out about them all."

"You can't be serious. You have nothing on me. You have lost your mind!"

At that moment, the door opened and Sam walked in, followed by a tall, slim, well-dressed lady. Staff's face went white and a look of terror came into his eyes.

"Jesus Christ," he muttered. "Sharon… you bitch… you promised…"

"Hi Warren. Long time no see. I just got tired of living the lie. And, the killing just keeps coming, doesn't it. Frank and I have been writing every since you killed Donald. We were both so afraid of you… all these years. But not now. It's over, Warren. I'm going to testify against you."

He couldn't speak. He slumped back in his chair and became limp.

Sterns spoke, "Sam, you did it again. Would you like the honor?"

"Yeah, I'd like that a lot." He took out his handcuffs and approached. " Warren Staff, you have the right to remain silent. Anything that you say can and…"

Chapter 92

Amber Street was on her way South on I-55 to Menard State Prison. She was happy, for more reasons than one. Beatrice had convinced her that Noah Ross was an innocent man, a victim of unfortunate circumstantial evidence that put him in prison for a crime he did not commit. That was good, because at their first meeting, she had become definitely interested in this man. Reading his manuscript, she was drawn as if by a magnet to his innermost thoughts and conception of what had happened to him. She felt his pain and frustration as he described his arrest, his trial and subsequent incarceration in this hell known as Menard State Prison. She also was happy that it was her privilege to carry with her the first copy of his first published book, *A Matter of Innocence*. Now, if only she could somehow manage to help set him free.

Noah was in a trance. He was staring at his life long goal… his first published book. It was a feeling of pride… of accomplishment… not unlike the feeling a first-time father has when looking at his newborn baby. *A Matter of Innocence* was, indeed, Noah Ross' first baby. He caressed it as one would a fine piece of cloth.

"Well, what do you think?" Amber Street was enjoying this moment tremendously. To be a small part of something so important was a special treat.

"It's beautiful. I can't believe that this is actually mine."

"Well, maybe this will convince you." She handed him the advancement check for $5,000.

"Wow. This is great! I never expected this much!"

"I'm so excited for you. You must be so proud."

"Yeah, I'm proud. I'm tickled to death! I wish I could take you out and buy you champagne… and lobster… and…"

She giggled. "You will someday. I will look forward to it. I took the liberty of opening a bank account in your name. I'll deposit it for you, if you would like."

"Yes. That would be fine."

"I'm holding you to the champagne and lobster promise. You will be free one day!"

"I hope you're right. I have less hope every day."

"Don't lose hope. That's the worst thing you could do."

"Yeah, I know." He was silent for a moment. "Well, what's next?"

"I ordered you a hundred copies… for signing, or whatever. And I have prepared a news release for the media. Beatrice and I think the book will help bring attention to your case. Maybe somebody has some information to help that didn't come out in the trial."

"Wouldn't that be nice?"

"That would be wonderful!"

"Would you do me a favor? When the other books get here, take this one and give it to my brother, Robbie. I'll sign it for him."

"Of course! You want him to have the first one?"

"Yes. I want him to have the first one."

"I'll be happy to make it happen."

"Thank you, Amber Street. Thank you so much."

Chapter 93

Amber Street was feeling good… feeling a part of something grand. She pulled her car into the lane leading back to Robbie's cabin, wondering why anybody would want to live in such isolation. On the seat beside her was a copy of a book. A book written by the most interesting man she had ever met. She had read her own copy three times already. It was a fascinating story.

She pulled up beside the pick up truck and stopped. The door to the cabin opened and a young man walked out. She got out of the car, standing close to the door.

"Are you Robbie Ross?" she asked.

Robbie was taken aback by her beauty. "I'll be anybody you want me to be, gorgeous," he flirted. "Who might you be?"

"My name is Amber Street. I'm one of your brother's lawyers. He wanted me to give you this." She held out the book.

Robbie left the porch and slowly walked toward her.

"What is it?"

"His book. His first published book. He signed this copy for you."

Robbie stopped in his tracks.

"Noah's book? It's finally here?"

"Yes. It's finally here. It's doing quite well." She was not expecting this reaction. The young man's eyes were darting here and there… full of fright. His mouth was open, but she could see it was difficult for him to breath. “Are you okay?” she asked.

His mouth snapped shut and he regained control. “I’m fine. Just fine. Give me the book.” He took it from her hand, turned and walked back to the cabin.

“You’re welcome,” she muttered, getting back into her car and driving away. *Well, that certainly was not what I was expecting. What a weird person.*

Chapter 94

Orville Merrell changed the channel to *Let's Make a Deal*, retrieved a diet coke from the mini-fridge, and relaxed in his new Italian leather recliner.

"Take door three, you idiot!" he shouted at the TV. One of the correctional officers stuck his head in the open cell door.

"Your visitor is here, Mr. Merrell. Do you want to meet here or in the visitor's lounge?"

"Bring him here, Charlie. Thanks." He took a drink of his coke. "Door three! Jesus, what a dummy!"

Money meant power and influence, and Orville Merrell had plenty of both. Even though he could not escape the criminal charges and the inevitable conviction, his incarceration was at the Statesville Correctional Center, a minimum security facility located in Joliet, Illinois. Other than not being able to leave the premises, he was able to have things pretty much the way he wanted, including a once a month conjugal visit from his *wife.* No one seemed to notice that his *wife* was a different woman each month. The stacks of twenty dollar bills he handed out periodically to the staff insured his stay would be, at least, tolerable. And he had no plans on being here for his full sentence.

He had a computer with access to the internet, a TV, a small refrigerator, and officers who brought him carry-out orders, including beer, wine and other essentials. He had also been able to continue to manage his law firm by telephone and computer. Other than his location, not much had really changed. Today, he was interviewing a man who wanted to join his firm.

James Truesdale… ex-Illinois State Attorney… paused at the cell door. "Orville?"

"James! Come in. I'm afraid you'll have to sit on the bed. I have only the one chair. Prison is hell, you know!"

He made no move to get up or to shake hands. He found the remote and turned the TV off. Charles Truesdale took a seat on the side of the carefully made up bed.

"Thank you for seeing me, Orville. I wasn't sure you would."

"You mean because you didn't do anything to keep my ass out of here?"

"Yes. I'm sorry about that, but I didn't have any choice. Sterns would have had me by the nuts if I had tried. We were lucky to get you here. It cost your firm a lot of money."

Orville's face hardened even more at the mention of Gordon Sterns. "Looks like he did you in anyway… the son of a bitch only won the election by three hundred thousand votes. How could you let him get control?"

"He had a lot of help. The FBI… that cop from Elmhurst… your ex-employee, the computer guy… a lot of help. I didn't have much choice, really," he pleaded his case.

Orville considered that for a minute. "You need a job, huh?"

"Well, yes. There are several firms interested, and I could even start my own practice, but I thought perhaps you…"

"Why should I hire you?"

"I know the system, Orville. If anybody can get your sentence cut even shorter and get you out of here sooner, it would be me."

"Perhaps," he nodded, pausing to think. "I'm not sure I can trust you, James. There are a lot of things that go on in my office that certain people would not understand. Most of the time the firm doesn't actually break the law... but we are often pretty close to it. You know what I mean?"

"Yes, of course. I understand that."

Orville punched a button and Monty Hall appeared back on the screen. "Ever watch this show, James?"

"No, not really."

"I've guessed the right door or the right curtain, the one with the biggest prize, thirteen times is a row. You know how I do that?"

"No, Orville... I don't."

"Instinct, that's all. I just get a feeling." He took a drink of his soda. "You want a job? I'll tell you what. You take care of a little matter for me and I'll give you a job. I'll make you a partner, even. But it's got to be done carefully. There can be no possible way anything can come back to me or the firm. My instincts tell me you could probably handle that. You interested?"

"What do you want me to do, Orville?"

Chapter 95

The painter was finishing the last letter of the name on the office door window. Gretch Investigations. Beatrice had agreed to rent him an empty office in her building and to let her receptionist take his calls and messages when he was out.

Sam put an ad in the Tribune and the Sun Times, called the phone book company to have his ad in the next issue, and gave the new Chief of Police his two week's notice. A young officer named Brent August was promoted to detective and was to take over all Sam's duties and open cases. His new career was off to a fine start.

Bebe had been right. He immediately began to get calls from other attorneys who needed his skills. Find this witness, locate this missing heir, and a variety of other tasks that any trained policeman could have done. But it was different. He was working for himself. He didn't take any orders from anyone… except Bebe, of course, and her orders were usually of a personal nature.

Orville Merrell was a brilliant lawyer. Only his failed knowledge of computer hard drives was a near career ending mistake. As with most people who have a layman's understanding of the issue, he assumed that when an e-mail was deleted, it was *deleted.* Bad mistake… one he would never make again. After his arrest and conviction, an event he was not prepared for, he now wanted one thing more than anything else. Even more than his freedom. He wanted revenge.

It was easy for a man with his contacts to arrange for a person's death. He had done it four times, the last being his communications manager, Lawrence Coverett. He could do it again if he wished, but this time, he had other plans. Killing Gordon Sterns, the new State Attorney of Illinois, would be good. Real good. But, no, he didn't want Gordon Sterns dead. Not just yet. He wanted him destroyed first.

"Sam… you better come over to my office as soon as you can."

"Now what, Bebe? You okay?"

"I'm fine, honey. But you need to come over. It's important."

"Be right there." He closed the file he had been reading and walked down the hall to Bebe's office.

The receptionist told him to go right in. He was mildly surprised to find Robbie Ross sitting across from her.

"What's up?"

"You had better sit down. We have news." That would prove to be an understatement.

Robbie had been talking for fifteen minutes. It was quite a story.

"I don't believe you. You were in Minnesota, remember?" Sam reminded him.

"Not till after. I drove there after the shooting. The guys in Minnesota… they'll lie about anything for a few beers."

"Come on, Robbie. This is bullshit. What about the prints on the gun? They all belonged to Noah." Sam wasn't convinced.

"I took a wire… hooked it over the trigger. I just left it in the holster. I had to use both hands, but it worked fine. I didn't think about cutting a hole in the side."

"You really don't think I'm going to believe you, do you?"

"Yes, I think you'll believe me. The paper… in Pritchard's pocket. You still got it?"

Sam's head shot up. Very few people knew about the paper. It never came out at the trial because he could never figure out if it was connected or not. He had looked at it so many times he could remember all the numbers. "What about the paper?"

"If you add one digit to each number, you will have my social security number and the date of my birthday. If you go back one letter on the initials S.S., you will have my initials… R.R. Robb Ross."

Sam's mouth gaped open. "I'll be a son of a bitch." It was turning out to be a busy Monday. He was stunned… and confused.

"Why did you do it, Robbie? Why did you frame your brother and why are you coming forward now?"

"I know it sounds stupid, but I did it so he could get a book published. Then things got out of hand. For one thing, I didn't think it would take this long. Amber Street brought me a copy of his book. I need to get him out of prison. It's time to get him out of prison."

"Why did you come here?" Bebe asked.

"I need an attorney."

"Well, it can't be this firm. Conflict of interest. Sorry."

"I can't afford to hire my own."

"Then I guess you'll have to take your chances with a public defender."

"Are you officially turning yourself in?" Sam asked.

"Yes."

"Okay, then. We'd better go to the police station."

Chapter 96

Noah Ross was dreaming. He was in a field of wild flowers, barefoot, sitting at his desk pounding away at the keyboard on his computer. It was a glorious, warm day and the gentle breeze carried the wonderful scent of the flowers around his head in a soft caress. Suddenly, there was a door to his right. It opened up and Miss Amber Street entered. She was beautiful… dressed in a flimsy, silk, clingy thing, the color of lilacs. Her hair glowed in the sunlight and at that moment, he knew he loved her. Oh, how he loved her.

"You're free, Noah." She said softly. "You're free. Come with me. Let me show you my love…"

The loud bang of the cell door slamming open rudely woke him. "Showers today, children. Out the door in five, please." The voice belonged to Andy, one of the nicer guards who had a God-like deep voice that made one wonder where it came from.

"Damn it, Andy… I was having a great dream!" Noah complained.

"Don't make the rules, Bible Noah. I jus' makes ya follow 'em." His remark was followed by his likeable laugh as he went on down the cellblock.

After his shower and breakfast, he was back at the computer, only this time there were no flowers and no Amber Street.

"What you working on now, Noah?" Harley asked from around the corner.

"The warden's autobiography."

"Isn't an autobiography supposed to be written by the subject?"

Noah chuckled. "Tell that to the warden."

"Oh, I see. So this was not a voluntary thing on your part. Now, I understand."

"Actually, it's my punishment for not seeing anything when the General was killed."

"Ross… you got visitors," the guard interrupted. "You know the drill. Let's get you chained up."

He was disappointed to find Beatrice Martin and Sam Gretch waiting for him in the *cold room*. He had hoped it would be Amber.

"You two come for the morning tea?"

"We have some very good news for you Noah. However, we also have some very bad news," Beatrice started.

"Good news-bad news joke? You want to know which I want first?"

"I'm afraid there's nothing funny here, Noah." Sam added.

"Then just tell me. Everything at once."

Beatrice took a deep breath. "The real killer of John Pritchard came forward yesterday and confessed."

Noah stared at her face to make sure she was serious. His heart was in his mouth. "I did hear you correctly? John Pritchard's killer?"

"Yes, you heard correctly."

"Well, there sure as hell can't be any bad news, then!"

Sam spoke up. "Hold on, Noah. This is not going to be easy. The man who really murdered Pritchard was… your brother. Robbie."

Noah's eyes narrowed and he drew back. "Oh, come on! You can't be serious!"

"We're serious, Noah. Robbie killed John Pritchard. He had information about the shooting that only the killer would know. He did it. He said he did it for two reasons. First, he found out that Linda was having an affair with the deceased and the other reason was... he wanted to frame you for the murder so you would be famous enough to get a book published." Beatrice paused to let it all sink in.

Suddenly, a scene was replaying in his mind. He and Robbie were out on his deck, sharing a beer and talking about his futile efforts to get a book published. "You have to be famous or kill somebody" he had said. "Okay, bro... hang in there... I'll think of something." Robbie had replied.

"My God. He really did it. Stupid assed kid! He really did it."

"Yes, Noah... he really did it." Beatrice said sympathetically.

Chapter 97

Robbie waived his right to a trail, preferring to go before a judge. He readily admitted to killing John Pritchard and pled guilty to first degree murder. It didn't take but four hours for the judge to accept his guilty plea. As soon as the verdict was rendered, Gordon Sterns filed papers to have Noah released. The news made the front page of all the Chicago newspapers.

"So, you're leaving me, friend?" Harley asked. The two men were seated alone in the rear of the mess hall, having dinner.

"I will miss you, Harley… but yes… I'm leaving you. My attorney says the papers will be ready tomorrow."

"So this is our last supper. I believed you, Bible Noah… when you said you were innocent. I was one of the few."

"I know, friend. I know."

"Will you keep writing?"

"I don't know, Harley. Maybe…maybe not. My brother did a stupid thing. An unbelievable thing. He paid a high price to get me published. I'm not sure what to do about that."

"You will. It may take some time, but you'll figure it out."

"I hope so, Harley. I hope so."

They were interrupted by several inmates banging on their plates with spoons. The head of the black gang known as Blood and Balls, a fellow nicknamed Crazy Ike, stood and begin speaking in a loud voice.

"Lissen' up! Fellow losers and otherwise worthless assholes… I hear we are losin' one of own. But then, he was not really one of own, now was he? Perhaps that is the reason I am happy to see him go. Normally, I wouldn't give a shit, one way or the other, but Bible Noah has brought a level of dignity to our cellblock that most of you shitheads didn't even recognize. I, for one… wish him good luck."

Slowly, he started clapping his hands. Whap. Whap. Whap. Then the beat increased as the other inmates joined in, and soon, every one in the room was clapping as hard as they could. It was an eerie moment that Noah would never forget. Never.

The guard unlocked the gate at 1:00 p.m. and Noah stepped out into the sunlight. He was not expecting the sight that greeted him. There were several hundred people gathered in the parking lot. At least thirty reporters, TV crews from all the major networks, Sam and Beatrice, of course, and representatives from the State Attorney's office, and a group demonstrating against wrongful imprisonments… all cheering and clapping. He was overwhelmed. Then he saw her. She was standing behind Beatrice…as if uncertain if she should come forward. He started to approach her.

"How does it feel to be free?" a man yelled, thrusting a microphone in his face.

"Any hard feelings, Mr. Ross?" another asked.

"What's the first thing you're going to do?"

"Are you going to sue the State?"

Noah stopped and smiled. "Gentlemen… and ladies. I will make a statement in a minute. Please be patient. First, let me get through to my friends."

The crowd quieted and parted, giving him access. With definite purpose, he walked straight to Amber, took her hands in his own and looked into her face. She was crying… tears of joy.

"We have business… you and me, Amber Street."

"Yes, Mr. Ross. We do, indeed."

"Give me a moment, will you?"

"Of course, Mr. Ross. Take all the time you need."

"Thank you." He let go of her hands and turned to Beatrice as a grin came across his face. He took a deep breath and hugged her tightly. "My loyal counselor… thank you so much." He released her and faced Sam. "And Detective Gretch… it will take me a little while to fully realize what has happened. When I do, maybe I'll find the words to properly thank you. Right now, I don't know what to say… except that. Thank you."

"Don't you hug me," Sam teased.

Noah smiled and offered his hand. "No… no hug for ugly people," Noah teased back. "I guess I need to say something to my fans, huh?"

"That would be a good idea," Beatrice offered.

He turned and faced the crowd. "Thank you all for coming. Some of you had to come… since it's your job. Others… others are here for a variety of reasons, many of which I probably won't understand.

Okay. So, I was falsely accused and convicted of murder. I've had a lot of time to think about that. Three years, two months, seven days and four hours, if you really want to know. I've reviewed the evidence presented so aptly by the prosecuting attorneys. And I have thought at great length of the defense presentation, so aggressive, even though there was not much to present except for my word. I have come to the conclusion that had I been on the jury… I would have found the defendant guilty as well. So there's nothing to be gained by any court action on my part… and I will be forever thankful that I am now free. As you all know, my brother has confessed to the crime. As you might well imagine, I am confused and greatly saddened by this. Perhaps I will never understand the motives for his actions. I will pray for his soul… and I ask that you all do the same. That's all I have to say." He turned to his friends. "Let's get the hell out of here!"

Chapter 98

"What would you like for dinner, Noah? I'm treating," Sam asked. The four were in Sam's car on the interstate heading back north to Elmhurst. Noah glanced at Amber, grinned and said, "A really greasy hamburger… with raw onions and a beer!"

"I know just the place!" Sam replied.

"Garlands. I knew it would be Garland's," Beatrice chimed in.

"I've never been there," Amber said.

"We don't go there much… only every day." Beatrice laughed.

"Garland's sounds great. I haven't been in there for over three years!" Noah announced. Everyone had a good laugh. "How's Robbie?" The mood changed to serious.

"He's in Cook County, waiting for sentencing… next Tuesday. I guess he's doing as well as he can. The court appointed Bernie Horton to defend him. He didn't have to do much work, since Robbie pleaded guilty," Beatrice responded.

"Wasn't he Linda's lawyer?"

"Yes."

He was silent for a minute…thinking. "Will it be possible for me to see him?"

"I think I can arrange that. Let me make a few calls." She paused. "Oh, by the way, he gave Amber the key to his cabin. Said to tell you since he wouldn't be needing it, and you didn't have anyplace to stay, it was your cabin now."

Noah shook his head. “I can’t believe he really did it.”

Amber reached over and in a sympathetic gesture, took his hand in her own. Like two teenage kids on a first date, they continued to hold hands all the way to Elmhurst.

The burgers were great. Jake made a liar out of Sam, refusing to take any money for the food and the beer.

“Jake got you off the hook… but you still owe me a dinner!” Noah reported to Sam.

“Anytime, bud. Anytime!”

“Well… is somebody going to take me home? I’ve had enough beer.”

“I would like to do that,” Amber offered.

“I was hoping you would.”

“Come on, Bebe. Let’s get out of here and let these two get to know each other.” Sam rose and pulled Beatrice up after him.

“Hey, Noah… will you sign one of your books for me?” Jake asked.

“Sure thing, Jake. I’ll bring it by tomorrow.”

The lights flooded the living room in the cabin, greeting Noah to a sight he had never seen before. The room was neat and orderly… and didn’t smell like stale beer cans.

“Wow. I’ve never seen this place cleaned up before.”

“I did it yesterday. I wanted you to have a nice homecoming,” Amber said softly. “I washed the sheets and towels and… well, you know. Here’s the key…”

“Thank you,” he interrupted. “Would you…would you mind if I kissed you?”

She answered by rushing into his arms. Slowly, their lips met in a tentative exploration, then parted, nibbled and finally, consumed.

"Will you stay with me tonight?" Noah breathed.

"Just try and make me go."

"Did you want me to sleep on the couch?"

"Only if I can sleep there too."

"I was kidding."

"You'd better be."

Chapter 99

At two o'clock the next afternoon, Beatrice picked the two of them up at the cabin and drove to the Cook County Jail.

"A judge I know owed me a favor. You only have fifteen minutes, though, Noah," Beatrice informed him.

"Thanks. I appreciate that." They rode most of the way in silence, Noah's thoughts switching back and forth between the enormously wrong thing his brother had done… and about the best night he had ever had in his entire life. Quite a contrast.

The jail brought back instant memories, still very fresh in his mind. *You're just beginning, Robbie. You've no idea what you're in for.*

The interview room was similar to the one he was accustomed to. A steel table, bolted to the floor with a ring welded to the top. He was seated several feet away from the table.

Robbie was brought in, chained and shackled. *Been there, done that.*

"You have fifteen minutes, sir," the guard informed him. "Would you like me to stay in the room?" He handcuffed Robbie's wrists to the steel ring on the table.

"No, that's fine, officer," Noah said softly.

For a long minute, the two stared at each other without talking. Finally, Noah asked, "Why, Robbie? Why?"

Robbie shrugged his shoulders. "I… I love you, Noah. I was never going to be anything but a tree trimmer. You on the other hand… you have always been destined for… something special. Greatness, maybe. I wanted to be part of that somehow."

"I'll never understand."

"I know. I don't expect you to."

Noah paused. "You knew about Linda and Pritchard?"

"Yeah. I ran into them over in a bar in Wheaton. They didn't see me. I followed them to a hotel. I couldn't believe she was screwing around on you. She left the car unlocked, so I was looking around in the car for something to prove to you she was… well, I found your gun. I thought about killing her… but I knew I couldn't do that. Then I thought about what you said that day on your deck… about killing somebody to get your book published. So I got the idea to kill Pritchard and make people think you did it. He was an ass anyway. Actually, it was easier than I expected."

Noah was shaking his head in disbelief. Tears fell down his cheek. "You dumb kid. You've ruined your whole life."

"Yeah, maybe. But, look what I've done for yours. You'll be even more famous now. I've given you the material for your next book. The one where I get to be the main character."

"I won't write it!" Noah snapped.

Robbie grinned. "Yes you will, bro. It's too good a plot to pass up. Truth is always stranger than fiction. Didn't you tell me that once?"

"Probably… but it wasn't an original statement."

"Don't matter. It'll make a hell of a story."

Chapter 100

That Sunday morning in late August was bright and sunny. The two couples pulled into the parking lot at Wilmette Harbor, put the coolers in the boat, and Sam begin to back his huge prize down the ramp into the water. Their maiden voyage. They were interrupted by the uniformed marina manager.

"Sir, you have to register and obtain a docking permit before you can put in here."

He was writing the name of the boat on a form attached to his clipboard.

"No problem. How much is the permit?" Sam asked.

"Fifty dollars for the year, sir. If you will step into the office and fill out the form?"

"Hold on, guys. I'll be back in a minute," Sam announced and followed the man inside the small office next to the ramp.

Beatrice, Amber and Noah took a seat on a bench next to the water.

"This is going to be great! What a wonderful day," Amber offered. She was radiant, dressed in shorts and halter top, covering her very brief bikini.

"Oh yes, this going to be so much fun!" Beatrice agreed. "Just look at that water!"

"Yeah. I must admit this is a lot better than being in prison," Noah stated.

Suddenly, a police car, with lights flashing, came to a stop beside the boat and two Chicago Harbor Police officers emerged and entered the small office.

"What the hell is going on?" Noah asked.

They didn't have long to wait to find out. The two officers returned, bringing with them a dangerous fugitive… Sam Gretch… in handcuffs.

"We've been waiting on you for a long time, Mr. Frost. Did you think we wouldn't find out who owned the boat? You are under arrest for operating a watercraft under the influence of alcohol and for fleeing police. Our supervisor is on his way."

"But, I'm not Jimmy Frost!" Sam complained. "My name is Gretch. I'm a private detective!"

"Tell it to the Harbor Master. The boat there… 'Precious', is it? It says you're Jimmy Frost."

They could all hear the siren coming closer and closer until the bright red police vehicle came sliding to a stop.

The officer stepped out into the sunlight and walked up to Sam, stretching to obtain his maximum height.

"I'm Sergeant Billings. Remember me?"

"No, sir." That was a lie. He did remember the man.

"I think you do. Nobody outruns me… no matter how fast your boat is. I always get you guys in the end."

"Sir, I wasn't driving the boat," Sam replied. "I'm not Jimmy Frost. Get these handcuffs off me."

"My memory's a little cloudy… but I think I distinctly remember you being the driver." He grinned. "Who's got the upper hand now, buddy? Nobody gets away from Sergeant Billings! Take him away, boys!"

"Wait! Wait! I'm innocent!"

"Where have I heard that before?" Noah mumbled.

"I'm an ex-cop! You can't do this!"

“Even cops have to obey the law,” Billings announced, sticking his chest out in pride.

The two policemen held Sam’s head down and put him in the back seat, then quickly sped away.

“What was that all about?” Beatrice asked, frantically.

“I don’t have a clue,” Noah said quietly. “Can either of you drive the boat?”

“Does he need a lawyer?” Beatrice asked the sergeant.

“Nah. I’ll let him go in an hour or so.” He laughed. “Just getting a little payback for my earlier embarrassment. What happened to that Frost guy… the one that was really driving?”

“He’s dead. He was murdered.” Beatrice said softly.

“Really?” Sergeant Billing’s fun was suddenly over. The broad smile had left his face.

”You any relation to Barney Fife?” Noah asked.

“That ain’t funny. I’ll go get your friend and bring him back. I didn’t know the other guy was dead.”

Once the boat was on the water and drinks were in hand, the four friends relaxed and began to enjoy Sam’s new toy. They were about a half mile out and cruising up the north side, enjoying the many sailboats and taking in the wonderful Chicago skyline.

“I’m afraid to go south… that’s where we hit the sandbar,” Sam announced. “God, what a day that was. I can’t remember when I was so drunk.”

“I can. The day Jimmy died,” Beatrice reminded him.

“Yeah, you’re right. People told me I got pretty drunk that night.”

Beatrice hugged him tight. “Nobody blames you for that,” she replied tenderly. “I brought fried chicken and potato salad when we get hungry.”

“That sounds great,”

Noah responded. “Sam, can we shut the boat off and just drift for awhile?”

“Sure… that’s easy.” He turned the key to the off position and the powerful engine became quiet. The boat quickly slowed to a crawl.

“We have something to tell you.” Noah looked at Amber. “We’ve decided to get married.”

“I thought you would!” Beatrice said loudly.

“That’s just great!” Sam added. “Congratulations.” They were both genuinely pleased.

“That’s not all. My second book is being released next week.”

“Really? What is the title?” Beatrice asked, excitedly.

“Brotherly Love.”

“Well, let’s drink to a successful marriage and a successful book.” Sam declared.

“Here, here!” Beatrice added.

It proved to be a very special day.

Chapter 101

Amber and Noah had set the date of August ninth to be united in marriage. The ceremony was to take place in a small town just north of Cincinnati where her parents had lived for over forty years. Since Noah's only living relative was in prison, and the right side of the aisle would be a little sparse, the decision was made not to have traditional seating at the church. No matter how many times he tried to make a list of guests, Noah could only come up with two people.

Beatrice and Sam drove down the night before. "Have you ever heard of The Golden Lamb?" Beatrice asked. They had just passed Dayton heading south on I-75.

"The what?"

"The Golden Lamb. It's Ohio's oldest inn. I read about it in a travel magazine. It's in a little town called Lebanon and I booked us a room there. Twelve presidents have stayed there from Bush to Garfield. We're staying in the Charles Dickens room. "

"Really? That sounds interesting. How far is the inn from the wedding?"

"Twenty minutes or so.

"That's good. They have a restaurant?"

"Of course, silly. Guess what their specialty is."

"Lamb."

"Damn… you're smart!"

They arrived at the quaint hotel around five. There was no bellman, and the small reception area was crammed full of people waiting for dinner. Sam lugged their suitcases into the room and pushed his way to the desk.

"Sam Gretch. We have a reservation."

"For what time, sir?"

"Not for dinner… for a room."

"Oh, of course, sir. Gretch… yes…the Charles Dickens room. Please fill this out." The young girl found the register form and pushed it in front of him. "Oh, you have a message." She was impressed. She had never checked in a guest before that had a message waiting. This guy must be important.

Sam signed the form and took the envelope from the girl. "Where's the elevator?"

"We don't have an elevator, sir. The stairs are to your right. All the rooms are named. You are in the Charles Dickens."

Bebe had shown up at his side. "Here, hold this." He gave the envelope to her. "We have to use the stairs."

The steps were narrow and steep. They had been built in an era when function was more important than ease or comfort. But, they made it.

In the room, Sam dropped the luggage and collapsed on the old four-poster bed.

"What the hell?" he yelled.

Beatrice started laughing. He had nearly disappeared, sinking deeply into the feather tick and into the down filled mattress. His head appeared above the ruffles

"I could lose you in here. We'd better hold hands!"

Filled with the hilarity of the moment, she kicked off her shoes and jumped on the bed and rolled into his arms, giving him a sensuous kiss.

"Charles Dickens, huh? Wonder who else has had sex in this fluff."

"I don't know… but they can add our names to the list."

It was spontaneous, it was fast… and it was wonderful.

Sam was sitting in the nineteenth century high-back chair in his underwear, waiting on the bath-room. The bed was so soft, one could not sit on it without sinking nearly out of sight.

"What did you do with that envelope?" he shouted.

"On the table by the door," came the answer. "What is it?"

"Don't know. Probably from Noah and Amber."

He tore it open. It was not from Noah and Amb-er.

Call me tonight. 618-945-7137
I need your help.
L.C.

"Who in the hell is L.C.?" he muttered. Curious, he dialed the number.

"Hello, Sam. Thanks for calling."

He did not recognize the voice. "Who is this?"

"Lawrence Coverett."

"Ah, Mr. Coverett. I wondered if you were still around."

"They sent a guy to kill me, Sam. He almost did, but I got lucky. I didn't stick around to see, but I think I killed him."

"You did. I found the body."

"You? How did that happen?"

"It's a long story. How did you know where to find me?"

"I called the Elmhurst police. They said you retired… started your own agency. I called your receptionist and she told me where you were going. So, I left a message at the hotel." He paused. "You did good, Sam. With the e-mails. Convictions on all of them. Great. Too bad they didn't get the proper sentences."

"Yeah, well, the credit should all go to you."

He dismissed that thought. "Orville is coming after me."

"Orville is in prison."

"Yeah, like that makes a difference. I need your help, Sam. Otherwise…"

"How do you know he's coming after you?"

"Because he can… and because he always wants revenge. There's no other reason for the attack at my apartment. I tried to go back there and get some stuff, but somebody is watching the place. It has to be Orrville!"

"From prison?"

"You call that a prison? He can get anything money can buy in there."

"Okay, let's assume you're right. What can I do?"

"Make him stop. I've been moving every week… so whoever he sends next can't find me. If he does, I might not be so lucky the next time."

"What makes you think I can make him stop?"

"I don't know. You're my only hope."

"Where are you now?"

"A truck stop near St. Louis. I'll be eight hundred miles from here by tomorrow night."

"If I can do what you want… and I'm not sure I can…how do you plan on paying me?"

"I've got money. I had a good job, remember?"

Sam thought a minute. "Lawrence, I'll think about it. I got a wedding to go to tomorrow. I'll be back in the office on Monday. Why don't you call me on Wednesday? That'll give me time to see if there is anything I can do."

"Thank you, Sam. I'll call." The phone went dead.

Dinner was very pleasant. The restaurant was the kind of place the locals went to on special occasions… and the place where they always took their visiting guests. A couple with two young boys was seated at the next table. Sam nearly fell off his chair when both the boys ordered salads instead of hamburgers and fries.

"You guys don't like burgers?" Sam asked them.

""Sure we do, sir, but salads are better for you. Are you having a salad?" the older boy asked.

"No, I'm having the lamb." Sam answered, smiling.

"Baaaaaad choice," the younger boy said, to which they all burst into laughter.

"I think he set me up," Sam said.

"I think he did," Beatrice agreed.

Chapter102

The wedding was grand. It was obvious that Amber's parents were very wealthy. Or at least they had been...before the wedding. The reception was held on a paddle-wheel river boat chartered for the day to run up and down the Ohio River. A ten-piece orchestra played everything from Bach to Willie Nelson. The two hundred guests enjoyed a sit-down dinner of prime rib and Cornish hens and all the servings. The liquor was all top-shelf and no one wanted for anything.

Amber was glowing the whole time and Noah was still in a trance. A happy trance.

"You know, I'm having a hard time accepting all this," he whispered during a slow dance with his brand new wife. "Two months ago I was worried about bending over in the shower."

"You still might have to worry about that, buddy," Amber teased.

Noah laughed. God, it was good to be alive.

Sam and Bebe had just left the outskirts of Indianapolis on their way back to Chicago. Two more hours to go. The conversation had been sparse. Both seemed to be thinking a lot about private thoughts. Bebe broke the silence.

"It won't work, will it, Sam?" she asked somberly.

"What won't work?"

"Us... being married. It wouldn't work."

Sam didn't respond right away. He had given it a lot of thought lately… but had not come to any conclusions. "I don't know. Tell me what you're thinking."

"Well, the way it is now, we have an understanding. You have your career, and I have mine. They're equal, and they are a big part of who we are. I'm afraid if we were married it would be different. I would expect you to do things… different… like staying home with me when you had important things to do at night… or go on a trip. And you might want things to be different when it comes to my work. Like me staying in the office till midnight preparing a case for court. I know you don't like it now, but you tolerate it… and so do I. But if we were married, I'm not sure we would."

"I see. So, what do you suggest?"

"Why don't we just leave things where they are for now? Maybe, when we get to be eighty, we can think about getting married. What do you think?"

Sam smiled. "I think you are a very smart lady. I love you. If you change your mind, let me know."

"I might some day. I just might."

Chapter 103

Monday morning, he drove to Joliet and parked in the visitors lot at Statesville Minimum Security Prison. *I wonder how much Orville had to pay the judge to get sent here instead of to a real prison.* He locked his gun in the glove box, entered the building and asked to see Orville Merrell.

"One moment, sir. I'll check to see if he is receiving visitors." The female officer was pretty and her voice was warm and friendly. Not the usual type of person one encountered when visiting a penal facility. "Could I have your name, please?"

"Receiving visitors?" Sam was surprised.

"Oh, yes, sir. Our inmates are not required to see people if they don't want to."

"I'll be damned," he muttered. "My name is Sam Gretch."

"Have a seat, Mr. Gretch. I'll see if he is available."

Sam sat in the hard back chair, a smile playing around his tightly closed lips. *I'll see if he is available. What a tough penal system we have*, he thought.

"Mr. Gretch, one of our officers will be here in a moment to take you to Mr. Merrell's room."

"Isn't he in a cell?"

"We don't call them cells here, Mr. Gretch."

Orville was propped up in bed reading the Wall Street Journal.

"I'm a busy man, detective. State your business and don't waste my time."

"Good to see you too, Mr. Merrell."

Orville lowered the paper. "What did you expect? A hug and a kiss? You're the reason I'm in here, remember?"

"No… *you* are the reason you're in here, not me. Anyway, I didn't come here to argue. I just want to know one thing. Are you going after Lawrence Coverett?"

Orville's eyes shot up in genuine surprise. "Coverett? I thought he was dead."

"Why did you think that?"

"I was told he was dead." It was obvious he was telling the truth. Whoever he had hired to kill Coverett had told him it was done.

"By whom?"

"That's none of your concern. You may leave now. This visit is over."

"Whoever you sent to do it the first time botched the job. Now he's trying to cover his ass by doing it now. Call him off, Orville… or I'll personally go after your ass. I'll bet if I really try, I can find enough stuff on you to get you out of this Ritz Carleton prison into a real hell hole… where you really belong."

"Why would a small town, piss-ant cop want to get in a fight with me? One phone call and your boss will have you directing traffic."

"I don't work for the department any more. Call anyone you like."

Orville's eyes narrowed as he studied Sam's face. "I don't get it."

"I'm a private investigator now. Lawrence Coverett is a client of mine. Get this guy off his ass or I'll make your miserable life even more miserable. Understand?"

"Fuck you, Gretch," he growled, then yelled at the top of his voice, "Guard! Get this asshole out of my room!"

Sam smiled and turned to leave as the guard came down the hall. At the door, he stopped and looked back at the red-faced attorney. "Like I said… with my help and Coverett's computer skills… I'll bet we could really have fun with your files. Think about it." He turned and led the guard down the hall to the exit.

Orville Merrell threw the paper against the wall in a fit of fury. He had paid twenty thousand to have Coverett killed. A small price to pay for such sweet revenge. But he had been lied to. The job was not done. Coverett was still alive… and now, just as Gretch said, his source was trying to complete the job. Cover his ass was right!

"Mario, you son of a bitch!" he muttered, reaching for the phone.

Chapter 104

Mario Marrello owned a bar called Rooster's Tap at Harlem Ave. and 103rd. Although not actually one of the *Family*, he was a good friend of several members of organized crime, and was no stranger to countless low life scumbags who frequented his establishment, including prostitutes, car thieves, bank robbers and… killers for hire. Due to the nature of his business, he was also a good client of Orville Merrill's law firm. It was him who Orville had called on to take care of his ex-employee, Mr. Lawrence Coverett. Of course, Mario was not about to do the job himself, although he had killed three men in his time. No, it was too easy to hire one of his customers, a black fellow of some size, called Frenzy.

"I'll do anybody for two grand," Frenzy had said several times, bragging after a few beers. So, Mario paid him two grand to kill Lawrence Coverett, netting himself a profit of eighteen-thousand dollars. Instead, dumb ass Frenzy got himself killed, and Coverett was running around free. Knowing that Orville would find out sooner or later, Mario decided he'd better to get somebody to finish the job... quickly. So, he went where anyone who did not want to chance another failure went for such services… his friends in the *Family.* The cost… twenty thou. There went his profit and then some.

Equipped with modern day weapons such as computers, phone and credit card tracers, it was only a matter of time before John Santos would locate his prey. Then he would complete the contract and that would be that. According to his last credit card usage, Coverett was in a truck stop near St. Louis. John Santos was twenty minutes away.

About the same time, the phone rang in Mario's office.

"Yeah, talk," Mario answered.

"Orville Merrell, you scum bag. What did you do, send one of your stupid bar derelicts to take care of Coverett? "

"Well, I…"

"You lied to me. Said it was done."

"I know, Orville… I'm sorry. I got somebody else on it now. He'll take care of it for sure."

"No. Call him off. I don't want Coverett harmed, you understand?"

"Call him off? You serious?"

"Yes, I'm serious. Call him off… now!"

"But…"

"Call him off… and give me back my twenty thou. Today."

"Orville… I already paid the guy!"

"Your problem, scumbag, not mine. I want my money back, understand?"

"Y'yes. Of course."

"Good. Do it now."

Frantically, he made the call.

"It may be too late, Mario. What the hell is going on? Make up your mind, already!"

"I'm sorry, Paulie, but you gotta call him off… or I'm a dead man!"

"Okay, Mario. I'll try. We will keep the money."

"I figured that."

John Santos was parked next to Lawrence Coverett's car. The twenty-five automatic equipped with the silencer was lying on the seat at his side, and the passenger window had been lowered.

Coverett walked out of the restaurant into the night air and took a deep breath, pausing to look at the night sky. *I hope Gretch's talk with Orville did some good,* he thought. *I think I'll head for Rapid City.*

Santos watched as his prey began to walk closer. He picked up the gun and slid the safety off. His phone rang.

"Not now, dammit!" he muttered. "Not God damned now!"

Coverett stopped, trying to tell where the ringing was coming from. His attention went to the black Cadillac parked next to his car and he could see clearly a man in the front seat. Quickly, he turned and went back into the restaurant. *They've found me. Now what?"*

He nearly ran as he headed to the restroom, entered a stall, locked the door and sat on the seat, bracing his legs against the door. He wasn't going to go easy.

He waited, holding his breath every time the door opened and someone entered, relaxing only when he could hear the sound of a stream bouncing off the urinal. For a hour he waited. When he finally had enough courage to leave, he worked his way slowly around the restaurant building where he could see his car. The Cadillac was gone.

Chapter 105

Warren Staff was still in the Cook County Jail awaiting sentencing. He had been convicted of two murders. First, the killing of Donald Anderson, that had been witnessed by his ex-wife who came back to betray him after living all these years in luxury in a Memphis townhouse. The second conviction was for the death of Captain Frank Boldery. That one was based on forensic tests made on a Tootsie-roll wrapper and a fingerprint found on the back door of Boldery's car. On the advice of his attorney, he confessed to both, hoping to make a plea for something less than the death penalty. During the trial, it came out that Boldery had been responsible for Jimmy Frost's murder. The judge had set the date for sentencing in three weeks. Unfortunately, he didn't have near the funds that Orville Merrell had.

Chapter 106

Gordon Sterns walked the few blocks from the State Attorney's office to the Berghoff like he had done dozens of times over the last three years. It was his favorite restaurant for lunch. He was in no hurry today. It was Friday, the weather was warm and he had a rather light schedule, so he took his time, enjoying the breeze that had drifted in off the lake. He did not notice the brown van that passed him three times in his six block walk. *Click*. Nor did he notice the telephoto lens on the camera pointed in his direction. *Click,*

Inside the restaurant, he took a seat at the counter and ordered his favorite… a schnitzel sandwich and a bottle of beer. *Click.*

He wasn't sure when she sat down. He didn't notice her at first. But he did notice her perfume. Trying not to be too obvious, he slowly turned to his left to get a look. Unfortunately, she had turned the same way, looking at something to her left. Her blond hair was gorgeous, but her face remained a mystery. He turned back to his beer.

"This is not a pick up line, but do you come here often?" Her voice was low for a woman's. Intriguing.

"What?"

"Here… the restaurant. This is my first time. I was wondering what was good."

He turned to give her his complete attention, now. Her face was just as beautiful as her hair. *Click.*

"Oh, hi," he stammered. "Good? Oh, everything here is quite good. My favorite is the schnitzel. You should try it."

"Okay, I will," she declared, studying his face. "Do I know you from somewhere? Oh, my. Sounds like another pick up line, doesn't it?" Her smile was sensuous...inviting.

He smiled back. "Yeah… but that's okay. I've never had such a beautiful lady try to pick me up before. I'm Gordon Sterns." He held out his hand.

"Yes, of course you are! State's Attorney. You're in the paper all the time. No wonder you looked familiar. I'm Susan Morgan." She gracefully took his hand.

"Hi, Susan Morgan. It's a pleasure to meet you."

"Likewise, Mr. Sterns. I'm a graphic designer for a small advertising agency on the North Side. I don't get down town very often, but I had heard about the Berghoff. So… here I am… having lunch with the famous Mr. Sterns."

"Please, call me Gordon. All the beautiful graphic designers that I know call me Gordon."

She laughed. "And how many would that be?"

"One. Just one." *Click.*

Chapter 107

The faces on the couple sitting across from his desk reflected the pain and concerned they were feeling. Sam felt so sorry for them. *I hope I can help.*

"So you have not seen her for two weeks?"

"That's correct. We had an argument… about this guy she was seeing. He was… is… Arabic," the Mrs. answered.

"Our daughter is usually very level-headed, Mr. Gretch. Not like her at all. She flew into a rage and stormed out of the house. We've not seen her since."

Greg and Judy Harper appeared to be Mr. and Mrs. Normal American Couple. Only now, they had a problem. Their daughter was missing. No reason to suspect foul play at this point.

"Does she have a cell phone?" Sam asked.

"Yes," her mother replied.

"A credit card?"

"Yes."

"A drivers license?"

"Yes."

"Good. If you can call me with the numbers, that will be a big help. Did you bring a photo?"

"Right here." Her father handed over a four by six glossy.

"Okay, Mr. and Mrs. Harper, I'll get started right away. Most of the time, these things turn out okay," he said, trying to reassure them.

"Mr. Gretch, we… we are not wealthy. What is this going to cost?"

"Greg! It don't matter!" Mrs. Harper exclaimed.

"Mr. Harper, my fee is usually fifteen hundred a day plus expenses. I'll find your daughter for half that, you have my word," Sam declared.

"I can live with that. Thank you."

Chapter 108

It had been a long time since Gordon Sterns had had any fun. The job was extremely demanding and he gave it his all. His relationship with his wife these days was nearly non-existent. He did his thing twenty-four/seven and she did hers… whatever that was. Today, however, he was having lunch with a beautiful, sexy lady and that was proving to be definitely fun.

"So, Susan Morgan, what brings you down town?" he asked, between bites of his sandwich.

"I had an appointment with a client from down state. We met at his hotel a few blocks from here. He is on his way back to Carbondale by now."

"So, you're done for the day?" He wasn't sure why he asked that. Well, maybe he was.

"I am. What about you?" Her voice had lowered an octave.

"I'm married, you know." He didn't look at her.

"I assumed you were. I think all the men I have ever been interested in have been married. All the good ones, anyhow."

"So, that doesn't matter?"

"Of course it matters." She raised her head and looked at his face through her long eyelashes. "Are we going to spend the rest of the afternoon talking or are you coming with me to my hotel?"

"You have a room?"

"Yes. I was planning on staying downtown and seeing a show tonight."

Gordon paused for a moment. He was quite intrigued by this woman. Finally, he removed his cell phone from his suit pocket and dialed.

"Gordon, Anna. Call Mr. Bowker and reschedule our appointment for this afternoon. I just realized I have a very important situation I need to take care of today." He closed the phone and returned it to his pocket.

She smiled. "Can I help… take care of your situation?"

He returned her smile. "You caused it. It's only right that you take care of it." *Click.*

The Harpers had called in with the information on their daughter's credit card at 2:00 pm. By 4:30, Sam had discovered she had used the card three times in the last four days in Elkhart Indiana. He called.

"Mrs. Harper, Sam Gretch."

"Mr. Gretch… what did we forget?"

"Oh, nothing like that. Listen, do you know anybody in the Elkhart… a relative or friend?"

"Why, yes, my sister lives there. We aren't close, though. A long time family argument, I'm afraid."

"I think you should go there, Mrs. Harper. I think that's where your daughter is."

"At my sister's?"

"Yes. She has used her credit card three times in the last week and every time it's been in Elkhart."

"Oh, thank you, Mr. Gretch. I'll call right away."

"Mrs. Harper, I wouldn't do that. Go there. Find her. Make things right. If she knows you're coming, she may run again."

"Yes… yes, you're right, of course. I'll call you when we know for sure. Thank you so much."

Sam hung up the phone and leaned back in his chair, smiling. *Wow! If she's there, I just made seven hundred and fifty dollars for two hours work. This job is really easy.*

"Don't break your arm patting yourself on the back," Bebe teased. "You just got lucky."

"I know," he replied. They were having lunch as usual, with Jake Garland. One of the cops Sam used to work with came in.

"Hey, Sam. Hi Beatrice. How you guys getting' along?"

"Roger… good to see you." Sam replied. "We're fine. What's going on?"

"Nothin', Sam. Absolutely nothin! Things are dull as hell since you left."

"Yeah… right." Sam laughed.

"Oh, there is one thing. Joe Mulvaney is retiring."

Chapter 109

Sam said hi to the desk sergeant and headed directly to the stairs. It had been awhile since he had been down in the basement. He knocked on the door.

"Joe? You in here?"

The door opened. "Sam! Thought that sounded like you. What brings you back to the dungeon?"

"Heard you was calling it quits… going out to pasture."

Joe laughed. "Well, it's time, don't you think? Thirty years of sweeping floors… that's a long time."

"What are you going to do?"

"I'm not sure yet. I may get me a RV… tour the country. I gave them two weeks notice three days ago. They already hired my replacement. They're really going to miss me, huh?"

"Yeah, I know how that is. I really came by to thank you… for helping me solve those cases. But, I do have one question. I've been thinking about it a lot lately."

"And what would that be, Sam?"

"You knew… all that time… you knew what had happened. You knew Staff had killed that guy, and you knew Boldery and Jimmy Frost were in on the cover-up. You knew, didn't you?"

"Well… I had a feeling… but I could never have proved anything."

"Why didn't you come forward?"

"Not my job. I'm not a cop… I'm a janitor. Nobody would have believed me anyway. I couldn't trust any of the cops… until you made Detective. You think you picked out the cold case on Anderson by coincidence? Wrong. It was me that put the file on your desk. It was a long shot, but it worked."

Sam was in awe. His mouth was open as a silly grin came across his face. "You picked my cold case?"

"Pretty brilliant, huh?" Joe puffed up with pride. "How's your new career going?" He decided to change the subject.

Sam shook his head. "My new career? Oh, fine. I'm really enjoying it."

"Good. You deserve it." He stood. "Gotta go, Sam. Toilet plugged on the fourth floor."

"Okay, Joe. Keep in touch."

Sam watched as the man went through the door and disappeared around the corner. "I'll be damned," he muttered.

Chapter 110

Gordon Sterns took of his coat and poured his first cup of office coffee. It had been a quiet weekend. His wife was visiting relatives in Ohio so he had the house to himself. Now, he was preparing to face the usual Monday onslaught of work.

The stack of incoming mail was in the center of his desk, awaiting his attention. He picked up the ivory letter-opener his wife had given him for his birthday and began to open the envelopes. He was able to guess the contents of most, having received many envelopes of similar nature in the past. One envelope, however, caught his attention. It was a 9x12 manila with his name and address printed in large block letters along with the word PRIVATE in several places.

He opened the flap and took out a stack of 8x10 photos. Instantly, he was overcome with nausea. His hands shook, sweat broke out on his brow and his morning breakfast was in his throat.

“My God,” he muttered. “This can’t be happening.”

In the top photo, he was the star… spread out on the hotel bed, receiving oral sex while fondling his partners breast.

Each photo became more detailed, his face the focal point in each one. There was no way he could deny the man in the pictures was himself. He was not surprised, however, that his female partner’s face was completely hidden from each view. How convenient.

The last photo had a post-it note attached:

WE WILL CALL YOU

Good God, what in the hell have I done?

Chapter 111

Sam and Bebe enjoyed a late breakfast then headed for the office. They had spent the weekend doing exactly what they had wanted… nothing. This morning they felt rested and rejuvenated, each looking forward to attacking the tasks of the day.

Sam was doing background checks on some prospective employees of a small investment firm in Chicago when the phone rang. When his secretary didn't pick it up, he assumed she was most likely in Bebe's office, so he answered it himself.

"Gretch Investigations."

"Sam… Gordon Sterns. I need to see you right away." The tone of Gordon's voice alerted Sam. Something was very wrong.

"Gordon… sure, come right over."

"No… we can't be seen together. I'll meet you here in my building… third floor, Suite 304 in one hour. Make sure you are not being followed. Use the Randolph Street entrance."

"What is it, Gordon?"

"I'm in big trouble, Sam. One hour. Suite 304."

The line went dead.

One hour did not give him a lot of time. Bebe was with a client, so he left her a note and headed into the city. But not before he had put on his shoulder holster with the Glock 19, followed by his ankle holster with the S&W nine millimeter. Gordon Sterns was one of the most stable persons he knew. If he was worried, then there was definitely something to worry about.

Suite 304 had a *For Lease* sign on the door. Sam turned the knob and entered the empty room. He was ten minutes early.

The previous occupant had left behind an old desk and three ratty chairs. He pulled one over next to the window and watched the traffic below. A few minutes later Gordon came into the room.

"Sam, thanks for coming." His face was covered in sweat, his upper lip quivered and his hands shook as he pulled up a chair next to Sam.

"What is it, Gordon?"

"This." He handed Sam the envelope.

"Holy shit, what did you do?" Sam was looking at the photos in disbelief.

"I screwed up… big time. First time I ever cheated on Rachel. First time." The man was nearly in tears.

"Rachel is probably the least of your problems," Sam said softly. He read the note. "Have they called yet?"

"No. Not yet."

"Can we get a tap on your phone… without a lot of people knowing about it?"

"I don't know. Probably not."

"You have any idea what they want?"

"Not really. Maybe somebody pardoned… a conviction reversed… hard to say. I doubt that it's money. I'm not that rich."

"Revenge?" Sam held his breath.

Gordon had not thought about that. "Orville Merrell?"

"Could it be?"

"Yes, it could be."

"Oh, my…" Sam replied. *Would it never end with that guy?* "Okay… let me take these and see what I can find out… if anything. Tell me about the girl. Everything."

"Well, she was beautiful, of course. Tall and slender… well dressed, but not flashy. More business like. She was blond, but not true blond. She had a room at the Ramsey Hotel. Said she was planning on seeing a show and staying downtown overnight. So… we went there."

"That accounts for how they got the camera in the room. Go on… any details you can think of… moles, birthmarks… anything,"

Gordon shook his head.

Sam looked at the photos again. "What is this?" He pointed to a dark blue blur on the girl's left shoulder.

"I don't know. I didn't get a look at her back. Tattoo maybe?"

"Yeah, maybe. I'll enlarge it. Not much to go on."

"What should I do, Sam? I'm terrified!"

"You can't do much… till they call. Find out what they want. You have to tell Rachel, though."

"Tell, Rachel? My God I can't do that! She'll kill me."

"You want her to find out from somebody else?"

Gordon put his face in his hands. "That son of a bitch. It has to be him, Sam."

"We don't know that, Gordon. He got a hell of a break from Judge Guilder. That fucking prison is like a resort."

"Yeah, I know." Gordon stood and stared out the window at the street below. "I know it's him, Sam. He's found out…"

"Found out what?"

"My office is investigating Guilder. Seems there was a two-hundred-thousand dollar donation made to his foundation a week before he sentenced Merrell and the others."

"Wow… that's a bunch of money."

"Not for that group." He paused. "God damn it, there's got to be something I can do… to stop this thing!"

"Gordon, I'll drop everything else I got going and get on this right away. You let me know the minute you hear from them."

Gordon didn't reply. His eyes were glazed as he peered out the window. He appeared to be in a trance.

"Gordon? You hear me?"

He turned and faced the detective. "Yeah, Sam. I'll let you know. I'll let you know."

Chapter 112

Sam left the building and headed straight for the State Police Crime Lab on Roosevelt Road. Over the years he had cultivated several friendships with a few of the technicians there.

"Is Clay Swift in?" he asked the receptionist.

A few minutes later, he recognized his friend as he approached the lobby.

"Sam, good to see ya. What's up?"

"I need to use your photo lab, Clay. Alone. I have some very sensitive photos I need to analyze."

"You got it, Sam. Then you can buy me lunch."

"Deal. Lead the way."

Sam enlarged the photo with the blur on the woman's shoulder and discovered it was indeed a tattoo. He could make out the shape of a small devil with a halo circling his head. "Well, that's a bit of a contradiction," he muttered. "Must be five hundred tattoo shops in the Chicago area. Talk about a shot in the dark!"

He stuffed the pictures back into the envelope and went to find Clay. He felt a little guilty about wasting time, but he had promised his friend a lunch. *I guess looking up five hundred tattoo shops can wait a couple of hours.*

Gordon followed Sam out of the building and drove over to the Adler Planetarium on Lake Shore Drive. He parked his new Lexus and sat on a park bench where he could watch the sailboats coming and going in and out of the safe harbor. For three hours he sat there… staring out at the water… not moving... thinking. Finally, he made up his mind.

He drove back to the State Attorney's office, retrieved his briefcase, threw a few items in it and headed back out. Back in his car in the parking garage, he took out his cell and dialed the number. A woman answered.

"Rachel… Gordon. There's something I have to tell you."

Sam and Clay had a nice lunch at a restaurant in Oak Brook. Then he hurried back to his office to get started on checking out where the tattoo could have originated. He hoped it was not one that every tattoo house in the country had available. Probably was, though.

Chapter 113

Orville Merrill was genuinely surprised. Of all the visitors he might have expected, never in a million years would this guy be one of them. He nearly told the guard that he didn't want to see him, but his curiosity won out. *This should be very interesting*, he thought. *Very interesting, indeed.*

"Mr. Sterns. To what do I owe the honor of a visit from such a distinguished gentleman?" His voice was full of sarcasm, unable to hide his hatred.

Gordon smiled. "Orville the scum bag. How you doing, buddy?"

"I'm not your buddy. What the hell do you want?"

"I came to inquire about your photography skills."

Orville had not been informed about the set up. "What photographic skills would that be?"

"Here… I'll show you." Gordon opened his briefcase and approached. With a blur of unexpected swiftness, he withdrew the ivory letter-opener and buried it in the throat of his adversary. Orville was unable to avoid the move. He made a sound like a gurgling garbage disposal, grabbing the handle of the weapon, trying to dislodge it. His knees failed him before he could pull it out. He collapsed in a heap at the foot of his carefully made bed.

Quickly, Gordon turned and walked down the hall and out the door. He got in his car, opened the glove box and took out the gun.

“Son of bitch will not hurt anybody else, that’s for sure. You did good, Gordon Sterns. You did good.” He put the gun to his head and pulled the trigger.

Chapter 114

Three weeks had passed since Gordon Sterns killed Orville Merrell then took his own life. The shock was beginning to fade.

The two couples were enjoying the afternoon bobbing around Lake Michigan in Sam's boat. It was hot, but the wine was cold and the sandwiches were delicious.

"I've got news," Sam announced.

"Good news, I hope?" Noah asked. Bebe was filling glasses.

"Yeah I guess. Closure news, anyway… about my dad."

"Wasn't he murdered?" Amber inquired.

"Yeah. Eighteen years ago," Bebe answered. "They never caught the guy."

"Naperville cop called me yesterday. They got a letter from the guy… confessing. He lived across the street from us. Shot my dad with a rifle from his upstairs bedroom. Thought he was having an affair with his wife. He found out later that he wasn't, but I guess that was a little bit late for my dad."

"Why did the guy come forward now?" Noah took a sip of wine.

"He's dying… pancreatic cancer. He's in Hospice… two or three days left. Wanted to clear his conscience… or something like that." Sam smiled sadly. "I guess he'll face the head judge, soon."

"Well, we have some news as well. More of a happy nature," Amber claimed. "We're pregnant!" She was glowing.

"Really?" Bebe squealed.

"That's great!" Sam declared.

"We're so happy, aren't we, Noah?"

Sam was caught up in the moment, thoroughly pleased.

"That's the best news I have heard in a long time. I'm jealous. I want a kid. Bebe… you want to get married?"

She looked at him, confusion clouding her face.

"To whom?' she asked, winking at Amber.

The End

LaVergne, TN USA
30 December 2009
168598LV00003B/5/P